To Bud
in the Gitz

Tom Osmond
27 Nov. 14

RIMFIRE

RIMFIRE

TOM DIAMOND

Beaverhead Lodge Press

This is a work of fiction based on historical occurrences.
The characters and their actions have been created by the author.

RIMFIRE

ISBN 0-944551-73-4

First Edition
1 2 3 4 5 6 7 8 9

Beaverhead Lodge Press
H.C. Box 446
Burnt Cabin, Beaverhead
Winston, New Mexico 87943

Publishing assistance by

Book Publishers of El Paso
1055-B Humble, El Paso, Texas 79915
(915) 778-6670

FOREWORD

The Mogollon Rim stretches in an arc from the San Mateo Mountains of New Mexico to the painted desert of Arizona. The rim separates the highlands to the north from the canyons and mountains to the south. The Apache lived along its spine, the last North American Indian Tribe to live wild and free. Their death struggle against the encroaching Americans set the rim on fire and is the backdrop for this story of lives caught up in the turmoil and destruction of the last gasp of Indian sovereignty.

PIE TOWN
DATIL
MAGDALENA
LUNA
HORSE SPRINGS
APACHE CREEK
FRENCHMANS WELL
SAN MATEOS RANGE
RESERVE
PLAINS OF SAN AUGUSTIN
ADOBE SPRINGS
OJOS CALIENTE
CAMP SHERMAN
MOGOLLON
BEAVERHEAD
SAN FRANCISCO RIVER
MOGOLLON RIM
CAMP VINCENT
ROCKY CANYON
BLACK RANGE
NORTH STAR MESA
BURNT WAGON
RIO MIMBRES
GILA RIVER
SILVER CITY
FORT BAYARD

ROUTE OF THE NORTH STAR STAGE LINE

CHAPTER ONE

THE STAGE TO SILVER CITY

Reacting instinctively, Tis-ta-de rose, with bow stretched to its limits, and loosed an arrow at point-blank range into the chest of Billy Joe Humphries. The bow's force was so powerful that the arrow pierced the young cowboy's chest, ripped through his body, and protruded from the back with flecks of his ruptured heart still clinging to the razor-sharp obsidian head. Mercifully, he was dead before he hit the ground. Not so merciful was the fact that the young warrior's arrow had ignited the Warm Springs Apache uprising.

The events that culminated in Billy Joe's death began at three in the afternoon in the Town of Magdalena, Territory of New Mexico on July 7, 1876 as Butch Garrison and Jeff Bartlett, both burly heavy-set men, finished hitching the four horses to the stage in front of Levy's store.

"Well, that's done," said Jeff, looking up and down the deserted main street. The day was scorching with not a cloud in the sky. "All we need now are some passengers."

Butch checked his pocket watch. "Almost three," he said. He had waited until the very last minute, hoping for some passengers off the Socorro train that had arrived almost an hour earlier. Apparently no one was continuing on by stage to Silver City.

"Wait out here in case someone shows up. I'm going in to tell Rich Levy we're leaving on schedule, passengers or not." He stuffed the watch back into its pocket and mounted the thick wooden steps that led to Levy's General Merchandise.

The interior of the store was filled from top to bottom with merchandise, from barbed wire to bolts of cloth. Rich Levy made a comfortable living anticipating his customers' needs. And he added to business by also using the North Star Stage Lines as a delivery service for the ones who couldn't make the trip into Magdalena.

Butch waited for the small bell above the door to quit announcing his arrival then called out to Levy who was filling some boxes at the back counter. "We'll be leaving now, Rich. Got no passengers today."

"Well, it won't be for nothing," replied Levy, indicating the boxes and a rifle piled on top of the counter. "I've got some groceries going to the Lujans at Frenchman's Well and you need to drop off a carbine and two boxes of ammunition at the mailbox tree in Corduroy Flats."

By the time the supplies were loaded and secured the stage was fifteen minutes behind its departure time, something that Butch could not abide. North Star Stage Line had built its reputation on promptness and reliability, and he wasn't about to spoil the record.

He climbed the wheel and onto the driver's seat, took the reins from Jeff. "You ready?" he asked his shotgun guard.

Jeff sent a stream of tobacco juice spatting against the dry dusty street.

"I reckon," he said, wiping his mouth with the back of his hand. Then he caught sight of the two people emerging from the rooming house and heading their way.

He knew both the attractive young woman and the older man who was struggling with a valise and large metal trunk.

So did Butch who had also seen them. "Well now, ain't that a pair?" he said. "What in the world is Lil Garrett doing out here in the middle of the day with the likes of old man Hawkins?"

"Don't know about that. But from the looks of those bags Hawkins is laboring under, I'd say we got at least one passenger."

As they neared the stage, Lil smiled up at Butch and said, "I hope you've got room for me." Butch couldn't help noticing how her auburn hair shimmered in the sun. He also couldn't help noticing the taut muscles in her neck as she tried to keep her composure, and the smile, in place. As far as Butch could recall, this was the first time he'd ever seen Lil outside of the saloon where she worked. Certainly the first time he'd seen her in the bright of day.

Butch looked past Lil into the face of Lester Hawkins and saw the other man lower his eyes. It was plain as day what was going on. "You bet we have room," he said, smiling back at the young woman. With that, he moved quickly to the wheel and onto the ground.

After he and Hawkins had wrestled the trunk onto the boot in back of the coach and Jeff was stowing the rest of Lillian's luggage, Butch took the man inside. "What's going on here?" he asked.

Hawkins replied, "Abigail Wilson and that new school teacher got their way." He quickly related how Abigail Wilson's husband had paid him a visit the day before, reminding him that the mortgage on his boarding house was up for payment. "Lil was a good tenant. Never gave me any trouble. Always paid her rent on time. Oh, she had a cowboy stay over every now and then, but that's all. But Homer Wilson is the bank president, Butch, what could I do?"

"We're ready." Jeff called down from the coach.

"Be right there!" Butch yelled back.

"You tell her I'm real sorry, Butch." With that, Hawkins turned and walked back toward the rooming house. As he did, the front door of the building opened and a woman appeared in the doorway, watching. Hawkins saw her and lowered his head.

Butch looked at Abigail Wilson framed in the doorway. She was a stout, flowery-dressed woman with a smile on her face. Which shouldn't have surprised him since he had long ago concluded that there was no meanness like a woman's when she's put her mind to it.

Butch stopped at the stage window and looked in. Lil was dabbing at her eyes with a handkerchief. "Pretty dusty out here right now," he said. "Care for some water to refresh your eyes, ma'am?"

Lil smiled and shook her head. "I'm ready to go."

He climbed back into the driver's seat and took the reins. "Gee Haw!" he yelled and the stage lurched into motion. By the time it reached the end of the block a small dust cloud had formed and a dog gave a half-hearted bark as the stage passed.

Butch turned the corner and headed toward the railroad station on the slim chance that someone might be there. A quick glance told him otherwise so he turned the stage around in the middle of the street and headed back the way he came.

As the stage approached Main Street, the back door of the

bank opened and Homer Wilson, a pudgy man in his fifties, hurried out, waving at the stage. "Hold it, Butch! You've got two passengers!"

Butch quickly reined in the horses and watched the bank president run toward the stage, clutching a blue carpetbag tightly with both hands. Behind him, Martin Zacharias, a sallow man in his late thirties, had removed a key from his trousers and was locking the door.

Wilson reached the stage, turned, and called back, "Hurry up! We can't keep the stage waiting!"

The Chief Teller tried the knob and, satisfied that the door was locked, returned the key to his trousers and hurried to the stage. Unlike Wilson, he carried no luggage.

The banker looked up at Butch as he and Zacharias boarded the stage. "I'll settle our fares when we reach Frenchman's Well."

"You want that bag up here?" Jeff asked.

Wilson clutched the carpetbag even tighter. His answer was short. "Important documents," he said and quickly climbed into the stage.

Butch grinned across at Jeff. "This could get interesting."

Jeff sent another stream of tobacco juice onto the street. "I reckon."

The first thing Wilson saw when he entered the stage were Lil's legs and he slowly worked his way up from there. When he saw Lil staring back at him, he reddened with embarrassment. "What are you doing here? You didn't have to leave today." He caught himself, realizing that his words had betrayed him. "That is . . ."

Lil reached across and patted the pudgy hand that clutched the carpetbag. "Relax, banker. One day or two, what's the difference? I didn't need much time to think about it."

Wilson reddened even more at the touch. He jerked his hand from beneath hers and quickly eased his bulk against the opposite side where he wouldn't have to face her.

Zacharias took the seat across from them, he didn't mind riding backwards. Besides, he could study Wilson and Lil at the same time. It would give him something to do to wile away the time until they reached Silver City.

"You folks ready?" Butch called down.

"Yes!" yelled Wilson, impatiently. "Let's go! Let's go!"

As the stage lurched into motion, Zacharias glanced at Wilson. The man's eyes were closed and beads of sweat peppered his face, his arms were wrapped around the carpetbag clutching it tightly to his chest.

If Wilson's eyes hadn't been closed, Zacharias wouldn't have dared taken such liberty as staring at his employer. Had he done so he would have encountered those cold blue piercing eyes staring back at him. Wilson had put that piercing gaze to good use in his business practices. Many a person had settled for less rather than deliberate against the banker's frigid blue stare.

He glanced at Lil, admiring her body. He had heard the same tales as others. If she liked you well enough and her mood was good, the right person could bed her down. One thing about her though, she never took money. Even if some good-hearted soul wanted to leave her a little something the next morning, she handed it right back. No. Lillian Garrett might be a lot of things, but she sure wasn't a whore.

Zacharias suddenly felt uncomfortable and turned his face only to see Wilson staring at him with those cold blue eyes. But before anything else could happen, the stage suddenly ground to a stop.

Butch stared down at Marshal Doyle standing next to the hitching post. He was a tall, powerfully built man in his forties and he grinned good-naturedly at Butch and Jeff. "Sorry to stop you this way, Butch, but I've got to take a prisoner into Silver City. I didn't want to drag him in irons all the way to Levy's and draw a crowd."

"Sure, Marshal, glad to oblige." He looked around. "Where's your prisoner?"

"Wait right here." Marshal Doyle went inside his office and jail and emerged a minute later with a young man in his early twenties, shackled with handcuffs and leg irons. He stopped at the stage and tossed a 30-30 and two leather pouches up to Jeff before opening the stage door and helping the prisoner on board.

Before he entered, he called up to Butch. "The court's waiting on this fellow, so I'm obliged if you can make good time. You can draw down against a federal draft from Uncle Sam for our fares."

"Just get on board, Marshal. I'll get you there in time."

As Doyle got inside, Zacharias moved as far away from the shackled man as possible. Wilson perspired profusely completely bathed in sweat. It seemed to ooze through every pore, soaking his suit. Even the carpetbag bore sweat stains from his hands.

Doyle noticed Lil for the first time and was taken aback to see her sitting there, but said nothing. For her part, Lil offered a smile in acknowledgment of the Marshal's presence.

"How do ma'am, my name is Billy Joe Humphries." The prisoner bent forward until he was able to doff his hat. "As you can see, I'm not traveling under the most gracious of circumstances. But I always have time to be gracious to a pretty lady." He grinned boyishly and put his hat back on.

Lil nodded slightly and smiled in acknowledgment, then turned her head and looked out the window.

"You ready, Marshal?" Butch called down from the driver's seat.

"Yep," Doyle called back. "Let's get started."

Butch snapped the reins and the stagecoach rumbled forward, slowly picking up speed as it left the city limits of Magdalena.

The passengers rode in silence for the first few miles. Fighting the heat and dust that filtered through the open windows was enough to handle without trying to start a conversation.

Doyle glanced at the banker sitting across from him. He didn't know Wilson very well. Only that that man had founded the bank in Magdalena five years earlier with money inherited from his father who had been a prominent stockyard owner back in Chicago. Wilson also had the reputation of being a no-nonsense businessman.

"What did you do, close down the bank?" Doyle asked, his voice breaking the silence.

The sudden question startled Wilson and he unconsciously hugged the carpetbag more tightly. "What do you mean by that, Marshal?" His voice strained, his eyes darting toward Zacharias.

"Nothing much," said Doyle, indicating Zacharias with a short nod of his head, "I couldn't help but notice both you and your Chief Teller are traveling together and I don't seem to recall the bank having any other employees. So it must be pretty important business to take both of you away at the same time."

"Yes, that's it exactly. Very important." Wilson tugged his handkerchief out of his pants and mopped his brow and face, then removed his hat and wiped the sweatband, being careful to avoid the Marshal's gaze.

"Is anything the matter, banker?" Doyle couldn't help but notice Wilson's attitude. It was completely out of character for the man and provoked comment.

Wilson stuffed his handkerchief into his coat pocket and looked at Billy Joe. "If you must know, Marshal, I don't see why you couldn't have taken this prisoner on horseback, instead of forcing him on us in these confined quarters."

"Wouldn't be safe. Too many miles and too much could happen between Magdalena and Silver City. This way, I've got extra eyes and I can get a little sleep if I need to."

"Well, I just want you to know I'm holding you personally responsible for anything that happens," Wilson said. His voice carried an edge of peevishness.

Billy Joe laughed and showed the banker his manacles. "Yeah. I'm a real big threat to you, ain't I, banker? I might snatch that fancy carpetbag you're holding and run off with it." He grinned and feigned a grab at the bag in Wilson's lap.

Wilson jumped as if he'd been shot and clutched the bag even more tightly. "Marshal, control your prisoner!" he demanded.

Doyle looked at the smirking Billy Joe. "That'll be enough," he said. "Otherwise, I'll chain you to the boot and let you run along behind the stage."

The young boy just laughed. "You don't want to wear me out before the hangman gets a turn at me, do you?" He looked at Lil, adding, "They're going to hang me, you know. All because I defended my friend in a fair fight."

"You shot a man in cold blood after you and your partner insulted his sister. Doesn't sound like self-defense to me, course I'm not the judge or jury." Doyle said. "Besides that, you broke into Levy's store and robbed him. Maybe, if you hadn't been so stupid and gotten drunk and bragged about it, you might have gotten away with the killing. Problem is, you drew too much attention to yourself."

"Why, Marshal, you make me sound like a real desperado when all I am is a cowpoke trying to get by."

Doyle laughed in spite of himself. "Billy Joe, you and your friends have helped yourself to other folks' cattle all across this country. Matter of fact, I hear tell that the only time you really do any work is when you're rustling somebody else's livestock."

The conversation was cut short when Jeff leaned down and yelled through the window, "Butch said to tell you to grab hold and hang on, he's fixing to make up some lost time."

As Jeff relayed his message, Butch studied the vast St. Augustine plain stretched before him. Crossing it this time of day was hard on man and beast. But the animals were fresh and it had to be done. He was the head driver for the North Star Stage Lines and there was a schedule to keep.

"Gee Haw!" he yelled and gave the reins a snap, sending the stagecoach grinding forward as the horses picked up the pace. "Gee Haw!" he yelled again. They had thirty miles to cover before reaching the stage stop at Frenchman's Well.

Meanwhile, Martin Zacharias quietly studied Lil and longed to say something nice to her. But he couldn't. Should he try, the words would be jumbled, making no sense at all. Zacharias was that way with everyone. He simply couldn't communicate verbally. He was very good with figures and he could write quite well, two very necessary traits in the banking business.

However, the most important trait as far as the bank president was concerned was Zacharias' not talking. In fact, whenever Wilson communicated with him the bank president's words hardly demanded a reply since they were usually orders to do something. Those he could respond to with a nod or a single word.

But, he thought, stealing a glance toward Lil, he would like very much to be able to talk to her. He would tell her that he understood the hatred borne by Abigail Wilson toward her. For months the older woman had stormed into her husband's office after hours, cheeks flushed and eyes burning with envy, repeating the latest gossip about Lil. Zacharias couldn't help overhearing her and he often wondered how she was able to acquire such intimate details without having also been present.

But, he knew he couldn't say any of these things. Instead, he closed his eyes and pretended to doze, letting the heat and dust settle around him like a cocoon.

Sleep was the one thing Doyle needed most but it had to wait until Frenchman's Well. A bitter past experience with another prisoner had taught the Marshal a lesson about taking too much for granted and Billy Joe was desperate enough to try anything because he knew what was waiting for him in Silver City.

Doyle caught a whiff of perfume and looked at Lil. She was daubing from a small bottle onto her wrists. The act was simple enough, but there was something so intimate, so personal about the way she slowly applied the fragrance. In the saloon, her arms had always been bare because of her clothing. But dressed as she presently was, with a full blouse and skirt, her physical beauty was both hidden and hinted at. She had certainly made his two years in Magdalena easier to handle. Although only sharing an occasional drink with her, Doyle had become very fond of Lillian Garrett. In his years of law enforcement, he had come to know people. He had to, his life depended on it. And, whatever her mode of living might be, Lilly was a good person and deserved better. If he were only a few years younger . . .

"Hey Marshal, got the makings?" Billy Joe's voice interrupted his thoughts. Which was just as well. They weren't going any further in that direction.

Doyle fixed the prisoner with a cold gaze. "Can't you see there's a lady present?"

Lilly heard the comment and smiled at the Marshal. "Thank you Marshal Doyle. But if he has a need to smoke, I don't mind."

Billy Joe's smile was almost sincere. "Thank you ma'am. You have a generous heart. But, I believe I'll wait awhile longer."

The banker swallowed bile as he watched and heard the deferential exchange. He couldn't believe what was happening. And, in any other circumstances but the present one, he would have made his dissatisfaction known, yes indeed. After all was said and done, he still might do so. Satisfied with that thought, he clutched his carpetbag a little more tightly and turned his gaze outside. But not before he caught Zacharias staring at him from beneath half-closed eyes. Had there been any other way, Wilson wouldn't have brought the man along.

"Seven o'clock." He heard the Marshal's voice. "Frenchman's Well by midnight."

Five more hours, thought Wilson. He closed his eyes and tried to settle into the hard seat, but his protesting bladder kept forcing him to change positions, an act made all the more inconvenient by having to shift the carpetbag each time as well.

He had finally managed to find a comfortable position when the aroma of Lilly's perfume drifted into his nostrils, and he found himself wondering if she also daubed it between her full breasts. Before he could wonder further Abigail Wilson's hatchet face appeared before him and any other thoughts he might have had withered on the vine.

Butch called to the passengers, "Brace yourselves," as the stage slowed and turned left onto the new military road that cut the Warm Springs Apache Homeland in two.

CHAPTER TWO  FRENCHMAN'S WELL

As Lieutenant Emery Whiting made the rounds of the corral and barn behind the stage depot, he gave thanks for the full moon and the immediate flat, open prairie land. He had a remuda of thirty horses corralled behind him, all bought from local ranchers within the past two weeks, and badly needed back at Camp Sherman.

At each small ranch where he had done business, there was talk of discontent among the Warm Springs Apache people. Once a friendly band, they had grown more and more aggressive in the past months, the culmination of years of constant encroachment on their tribal land, much of it sacred. Not caring about such things, miners scarred the earth looking for gold, silver, and other precious metals while the Apache was forced to look on helplessly.

In a sense, so was he. As a cavalry officer he was sworn to obey orders and to leave such decisions to others, unpleasant though it may be. True, he had his own opinion about the matter but he was wise enough not to volunteer anything. He would pull his duty and leave when the time came.

At the moment his concern was for the stage from Magdalena. It wasn't actually due for another hour. But if what those trappers had told Frank Lujan was true, then trouble could begin anywhere. And a stage in the middle of nowhere was a perfect target, especially under a full moon.

As concerned as he was, he could ill afford to send even one trooper to scout the situation. If the Apaches chose to attack the stage depot in an attempt to rustle the horses, he would need all the firepower he could muster.

"Lieutenant, sir." Sergeant Baskind emerged from the shadows.

"Yes?"

"The men are all posted as you ordered."

"Thank you, Sergeant." Whiting looked about him.

The night was peaceful, the only sounds came from the corral and, more distant, the cry of a wolf.

"It seems very quiet. What do you think?"

"Yes sir, it seems peaceful enough, but I'll be glad when daylight comes."

"The stage from Magdalena is our immediate concern, Sergeant. It's due at anytime. I will be much relieved to see it for several reasons. Passenger safety being the obvious first. Additional firepower, the second, should we be attacked." Whiting gave the area a final visual check then looked at the sergeant. "What do you say to a game of hearts until the stage arrives, Sergeant Baskind?"

"I would like that, sir ."

"Very good," Whiting replied as he started toward the rambling main structure. "Perhaps," he added as Baskind fell in beside him, "we can also enjoy a late meal of Senora Lujan's excellent cooking. I tell you, Sergeant, since I arrived on this assignment, I have become addicted to Mexican cuisine."

While Whiting and Baskind headed back to the rambling main house, Frank Lujan was finishing his chores in the barn. As he prepared the stalls for the incoming horses, he couldn't help thinking about the Warm Spring problem.

Lujan had come to Frenchman's Well from the Mexican village of Monticello. There, the people of the village and the Apaches had enjoyed mutual respect for many years. The Apache bartered pelts, hides, and sometimes turquoise in exchange for goods from the local merchants. On several occasions Lujan had visited their main camp only twenty miles away in Warm Springs, and was always greeted warmly.

Lujan's own nephew, Jaime De la O', had become fast friends with a young Apache named Tis-ta-dae. Both were fifteen and shared many interests, especially hunting. Jaime had accompanied the young Apache boy on several expeditions. He hadn't seen Tis-ta-dae in over a year, the length of his employment with North Star Stage Lines.

This thing, when it happened - and it was going to - would rest squarely on the shoulders of the Anglos. Almost without fail, they arrived as though they were already the landowners and everyone else merely tenants to be moved aside as whims dictated. To the Warm Springs Apache who had hunted these lands for generations, such acts were viewed as grave insults and showed disrespect.

People such as the two trappers who stopped by not only were greedy but also stupid. And to Lujan's way of thinking, stupidity and greed don't mix well. In the trappers' case, it meant not following the traditional manner. Instead, they destroyed the dams and slaughtered the beavers at will.

As for hunting, Frank had about given it up. There was a time only a few years earlier when game was plentiful. But no longer. The deer and elk had retreated to high country, distancing themselves from the miners' weapons. As for the wild turkey, he couldn't recall the last time he'd seen one.

While the miners feasted off the Apache's plate, the Apache was forced to eat the poison that passed for government food rations on the Warm Springs Reservation.

Yes, he concluded as he filled the last trough with oats, this thing will surely happen though it did not have to be this way. All because of stupidity and greed.

Lujan emitted a sigh, tucked the feed sack back on the shelf, then removed the lantern from its peg and left, closing the barn door behind him.

As he made his way to the main house, he encountered two troopers standing at the corral gate. Both were young and trying not to show their nerves. The nearest one reached and laid his hand on Lujan's shoulder.

"Tell me, amigo, does the Apache attack at night? I hear they don't because it's bad medicine."

Frank studied the boy. He couldn't be more than twenty-two and the look in his eyes said he wanted those words to be true. The other trooper was no different. Both green kids a long way from home and family.

But he wasn't going to lie. "The Apache will attack day or night. To him, it does not matter. What matters to the Apache is the situation."

"What do you mean, the situation?" the trooper removed his hand from Lujan's shoulder.

"If the Apache thinks he has a chance of winning, he will attack. If he doesn't think so, he'll wait until the situation is right." He stopped, put his finger to his lips. "Shh", he said.

He inclined his head slightly and closed his eyes for a moment and smiled. "Go and tell your Lieutenant that the stage is arriving."

Tis-ta-dae used the excitement to crawl away from the corral where he had been hiding. Nana's instructions were to count both the animals and soldiers. The animals had been easy, there were thirty horses, all fine stock.

The soldiers were not so easy. Only four had presented themselves. He knew there were more inside, but getting close enough to see was impossible. Especially now that the stage had arrived.

Nana's final words of instruction had been just as clear. "Avoid unnecessary danger," the Chief had said. "Do that which is possible and no more." As Tis-ta-dae snaked his way across the open space he heard the stage rumble into the depot and the driver's voice.

"Hey Lujan! Lujan! Stop sleeping on the job, we're here!" Butch yelled out good-naturedly.

Lujan was already waiting, waving the lantern as the stage turned the corner into the yard with Butch hauling back on the reins to slow the heavily breathing horses to a stop. "Whoa, now!" he said, "Whoa!"

Lujan stepped forward and grabbed one of the lead horse's reins, holding it steady. "I've got him, Butch," he said. With that, Butch stepped onto the wheel and down from the coach while Jeff did likewise on his side.

As they did, Whiting, Baskind, and the young trooper emerged from the main house and descended the stairs. "Trooper, assist the passengers," Whiting ordered.

"Yes sir," the trooper hurried to obey.

Butch opened the coach's door and stood aside as first the Marshal, then Billy Joe, exited. The banker was next, followed by Zacharias, with Lilly being the last to emerge. All showed signs of fatigue from the journey and the lateness of the hour.

When Whiting saw Lilly, he was impressed with her beauty and sense of grace, something that even the dust and exhaustion on her face couldn't conceal. But his immediate concern was the shackled man who stood next to the Marshal. With rumors about the Warm Springs Apache moving like a prairie fire, the last thing he wanted to see was another problem arrive. Unfortunately, such appeared to be the case.

"Sergeant Baskind," he said, "assist Marshal Doyle with his prisoner, then tell him I would like to speak to him privately on a matter of some importance." If Whiting elected to order the stage back to Magdalena, he wanted to have the lawman on his side.

"Very good, sir," said Baskind who headed to where Doyle had pulled Billy Joe to one side, allowing the other passengers to go ahead of them.

While he waited, Whiting moved further out of the passenger's earshot. After he and Doyle had discussed the situation, then he would make a decision and share it with the others. Until then . . .

"Evening, Lieutenant." The burly lawman approached while, behind him, Sergeant Baskind led Billy Joe up the steps of the stage station. Doyle shook Whiting's outstretched hand - firm but brief. Like all lawmen - or shooters for that matter - he never liked having his gun hand compromised for any reason.

"Good to see you, Marshal Doyle, for a number of reasons." If the rumors were true, and they were attacked, the more fire-power, the better.

"Same here, Lieutenant. Although I am kind of surprised to see a detachment of troopers. I thought you'd be in Camp Sherman."

"We've been purchasing horses from the ranchers for the last couple of weeks and finished today. I thought it would be best if we corralled them here overnight and set out early in the morning." Whiting paused, then asked, "Did you notice any Apache signs while you were on the road?"

"No, can't say as I did, why?"

"Word has it that Nana and about fifteen or twenty young bucks jumped the reservation and are threatening hostilities."

Doyle shook his head sadly. "Hell, I'm not at all surprised, they're treated miserably. But Nana is an old man. He must be nearly eighty by now and can't do much of anything. Besides, they don't have horses or weapons."

Whiting pointed toward the stage corral, "I've got thirty fine horses in that corral over there and you and I both know that weapons and ammunition can be obtained."

The Marshal was about to respond when Lujan called out from the porch. "Food's ready."

"Be right there, Frank," Marshal Doyle called out. "We'll talk more inside."

As they walked toward the house, the door opened again and Lil stepped outside. She descended the steps with that same easy grace that had captured Whiting's earlier attention.

"May I help you, ma'am? I'm Lieutenant Whiting, at your service." Whiting tipped his cavalry hat in respect.

Lilly smiled. "Thank you, Lieutenant. My name is Lillian Garrett, and I would like to have my luggage off the stage. I feel terribly dusty and soiled from the ride," she said.

Whiting smiled, "On the contrary, ma'am. You look as fresh as a daisy."

"You're too kind, Lieutenant Whiting. It's that large brown one in back," she said, pointing to the boot.

Whiting hefted the large bag from its spot and placed it on his shoulders, "This is too heavy for you to carry, Mrs. Garrett . . ."

"Miss," Lilly said, more quickly than she realized. "It's Miss . . . I'm not married."

Whiting smiled at the news, "I was wondering why a caring husband would dispatch his charming wife under these uncertain conditions. Nonetheless, this bag is too heavy for you. I'll be happy to assist."

"You're most kind, Lieutenant. Thank you."

Doyle watched them walk to the steps, the large trunk balanced on Whiting's shoulders. Once there, the officer still found a way to put his free hand beneath Lil's arm to assist her up the steps.

No question about it, the Lieutenant had a way with words

and, with women as well. He was a handsome man, exuding great self-confidence whereas Doyle could only wish that he had a little of both since he had long held strong feelings toward Lilly. Unfortunately, he was plain-faced and slow with words. Whiting had made that very evident. While he, Doyle, was trying to find the proper words, the Lieutenant simply spat them out with great ease.

Doyle watched them enter then made his own way up the steps. What he needed now was a good stiff drink to ease his aching bones and he was pretty certain that Lujan had a bottle stashed away somewhere. And there was always Billy Joe to deal with.

That's the problem with being a lawman, he thought as he pushed open the solid oak door. *We're so busy dealing with other people's problems that we never have enough time to deal with our own.*

Meanwhile, about a mile away, Tis-ta-dae had rejoined Nana and the others, recounting to them what he had seen and heard. When he had finished, Nana nodded his head then walked a distance away from the young warriors and studied the open prairie that stood between them and the horses they desperately needed. They numbered fifteen with only six horses between them.

His decision was critical. Of the fifteen, he was the only one who had ever fought. The rest were untrained and unseasoned. And, of that number, four were no older than sixteen and only recently initiated into the mysteries of the warrior path. He was responsible for their lives for he had chosen to join them in this thing. How else could he allow them to leave the reservation knowing the danger that awaited.

Nana knew the answer. The white man had no love for anything or anyone outside of himself. He claimed more and more of the Apache's land without understanding that it was a sacred gift from the Great Spirit. To be separated from their gift meant death to the Apache.

He turned to the others, saw the fear and expectation in their eyes.

"Tis-ta-dae has done well. And I have given his words much thought." He stopped and signed that they should sit on the ground in council.

As he curled his legs beneath him, he felt the years and age creep into his bones. One by one the young warriors took their places in the circle. Each face brought forth memories to Nana, for he had known not only their fathers but their grandfathers and great-grandfathers as well – leaders such as Mahko and Cuchillo Negro. How Nana longed for their wisdom and counsel this night.

His words came softly. "The moon is bright and there is no concealment, so you must be like the snake. They have rifles and guns; we have only our knives and our wits. Remember always, we came for horses, not lives. Do not let your anger make a fool of you. We are too few in number."

As Nana gave his final instructions to the young braves, Doyle, Butch, and Jeff sat at a large table in the corner of the way station sharing a bottle of Lujan's whiskey with Whiting, Lujan, and Baskind. Lujan had just finished updating the Marshal and the stage employees on the Warm Springs situation. Butch was already shaking his head. "Turn back?" He shook his head more vigorously. "Just because some thieving trappers had a tale to tell? No sir, I'm a North Star lead driver and I've got a schedule to keep." He turned to Jeff, "Ain't those your sentiments as well?"

Jeff scratched his head, looked around the table. "I never done anything to no Apache, so why should they be mad at me? I'm for going on."

"How about your passengers?" Whiting asked, glancing at Lilly sitting in the corner talking with Mrs. Lujan.

Although her English was broken, Lujan's wife enjoyed any feminine company that came her way. Then he looked at Wilson and Zacharias, sitting opposite one another. Whiting noticed that the banker, having been introduced to him earlier, still clutched that blue carpetbag. The only time it had left his hands was when he sat it on the floor between his legs while they were eating.

Zacharias was slumped in his chair, his hat pulled low over his eyes. Whiting had the notion that the eyes were opened and Zacharias was studying the nervous banker seated across from him.

"They have to be told," said Doyle, also glancing at Lilly as he spoke. "It's gonna' be their call, Butch."

"I agree," said Whiting, "I do have the authority to take charge in the event of a hostile situation."

"There ain't no hostile situation, Lieutenant!" Butch's pained expression was almost comical. "All we got is a possibility - possibility, mind you - that some young bucks are feeling their oats and jumped the Reservation. Hell, Lieutenant, there ain't been no one killed. There ain't been a single house burned. And most of all, they ain't got guns or horses!" He shook his head again. "Besides that, the Warm Springs have always been friendly."

"That's all well and good, Butch. But it doesn't change anything. I'm still leaving it up to your passengers. If they ask for my advice or request the military's protection, that's the way it will be."

"That's how I see it too, Butch." Doyle finished his whiskey then turned the glass upside down on the wooden table, a sign that he was through talking and drinking on the matter.

When the situation was posed to the passengers, Homer Wilson and Lillian Garrett found themselves in rare agreement. "There's nothing back in Magdalena for me," she said. The banker had already raised a ruckus about returning, all the while feverishly clutching the carpetbag. And Zacharias reluctantly agreed only after Wilson fixed those piercing eyes on him.

"Well, I guess that settles it," said Whiting, shrugging his shoulders in acceptance. Although, he had been pleased to hear that Lillian Garrett had no one back in Magdalena. He was smitten and admitted it. Moreover, he thought he perceived a reciprocal attitude from her. He couldn't be sure and, unfortunately, the moment was not right to pursue such matters. He would correct that at a later, and more opportune, moment.

"Hey! How about me? Don't I count for anything?" Billy Joe rattled his shackles. "I've had run-ins with the Warm Springs. I don't want to get scalped. Take these irons off me and give me a gun, Marshal. I give you my word I won't make a run for it."

Doyle glanced at the cowboy manacled around the large oak

post that supported the ceiling.

"Come on, Doyle, you may be going to hang me, but at least give me a little credit." He nodded in the direction of the door, "Just how far could I make it out there?"

"It's like this, Billy Joe," said Doyle. "If I free you and you escape, it's my rear end. If I free you and then have to kill you in the act of escaping, it's my rear end. Pretty poor odds if you ask me. Now, I want you to just be quiet unless I ask you something. Understand?"

Without even waiting for a response, Doyle turned his attention back to Whiting, Lujan, and the others. "So, what I'm hearing is, we grab what sleep we can and be out of here just at sunup." He looked at Butch. "What time would that get us into Camp Sherman?"

Butch's reply was immediate. "Around noon. Barring anything unusual, that is."

Doyle looked at Whiting. "Lieutenant?"

"My men and I will afford you all the protection we can. If we are attacked, we'll release the horses and that should end any hostilities."

"If that's the case, just turn 'em loose now and settle it." Billy Joe muttered to himself, but still audible to the rest.

Doyle fixed Billy Joe with a cold stare. "Billy Joe," he said, "if you persist in running your mouth, I'll be sorely tempted to chain you to the porch railing and let the Apaches use your sorry carcass for target practice. You'd best not try me any further."

Lilly watched Doyle handle Billy Joe. She had seen him at work back in Magdalena a few times and she had no doubt that Doyle meant what he said. Obviously, so did Billy Joe, for he turned his back and fell silent.

Lieutenant Whiting pushed back from the table and stood up, "Sergeant Baskind and I will post guards around the perimeter. The rest of you men find sleeping positions near a window. In case we are attacked, we don't want to lose time by being unable to return the fire."

He turned, singled out Lilly. "Miss Garret, I think you would be safer in one of the interior rooms. Mrs. Lujan will show you the way."

"What about me?" Demanded Wilson, who was seated nearby. "If she can have an interior room, then I certainly can!" he said. "I'm the President of the bank in Magdalena, while she's no lady."

"Banker Wilson," Doyle's voice cut in sharply, "I don't believe the lady was part of the discussion." He indicated a large couch against the far wall. "You can sleep there, it's big enough for you and your carpetbag." With that, Doyle turned and tipped his hat to Lilly. "Get some rest while you can."

Lilly smiled at Doyle. "Thank you, Marshal," she said in a soft voice, then accompanied Mrs. Lujan through the curtained archway and out of sight.

Whiting noticed the way Doyle watched Lillian Garrett. Even the Marshal's stern countenance couldn't hide his feelings for the woman. Having determined that, he decided against asking Doyle any questions about her. He would just have to find out for himself another way.

"I'll post the guards now, Marshal," he said. "And, I've decided that my men and I will bunk in the barn to give added protection."

As soon as the Lieutenant exited, Doyle extinguished the two lamps and took a position near one of the large windows. He could hear Wilson stirring and moaning to himself but nothing from Zacharias or Billy Joe. Which was just as well, he was in no mood for any more discussion. His hips ached and old wounds throbbed from the ride and the hard floor. Well, there was no going anyplace else so he stretched out, pulled his hat over his eyes, and decided to make the most of a bad situation.

By the time Doyle drifted into a light sleep, Tis-ta-dae and six others were within thirty yards of the corral, converging on either side. Nana had instructed them to start no battle, merely to steal the horses by freeing them. To do so meant that the gate had to be opened, which was not an easy task.

Tis-ta-dae had volunteered to be the one to open the gate.

He had been that close earlier and could have done so had he chosen. But, it would have failed because the soldiers and others were awake and near enough to stop the stampede. His problem was the sentry near the wall. It was almost impossible to avoid him if he was to reach the gate.

He stopped, gave a quick bird call, then waited. Moments later he heard the response, telling him that guards were posted on all sides. The flare of a match in the barn told him where the rest were.

A bird call signal caught his attention. It came from behind the barn. Moments later, two figures carrying rifles stepped around the corner, heading for the corral. When they reached the well, one stayed with the sentry, the other hurried up the steps into the station. Tis-ta-dae could also hear movement from inside the barn and knew the other soldiers were also awake.

As Tis-ta-dae signaled to the others, Whiting shook Doyle by the shoulder. The older man came awake at once, sitting erect, looking at the Lieutenant. "What's up?" he asked.

"We've got visitors. Listen."

Doyle put his head near the window. He heard the horses stirring in the corral; then he heard the bird calls coming from several directions. "Apaches," he said and was immediately on his feet.

"What do you suggest we do, Marshal? You're an old hand at this sort of fighting," Whiting said.

"First thing we do is wake everybody up. Then, we wait, Lieutenant. If they've just come for the horses, chances are they won't risk a fight. There are not enough of them, and they'd have little chance of escaping. I suggest you keep your men in place. Don't allow them to be drawn away from this area. The Apaches can sneak right behind a man almost, like his own shadow." Whiting nodded in agreement and left to instruct his men.

Mrs. Lujan, already awake along with her husband, woke Lilly and told her what was happening and then the two of them rejoined the others in the large room. They sat in the darkness and listened to the bird calls passing back and forth.

Meanwhile, outside, Whiting, Sgt. Baskind, and the two stage drivers were straining their eyes. They could hear them calling back and forth to one another and they knew the Apaches were within shooting range, but they couldn't see them, it was almost as if they were invisible. Whiting had already dispatched troopers to calm the milling horses.

Tis-ta-dae was near enough to hear the soldiers talking when he felt a touch at his shoulder. He rolled over quickly, drawing his knife as he did, when he realized it was Nana.

The old man placed his hand over Tis-ta-dae's mouth and signed for him to retreat. As soon as Tis-ta-dae understood, he began crawling away from the stage compound. Behind him, he heard Nana give the wolf call, their agreed-upon signal for retreat.

When the small band regrouped at the meeting place, Nana told them it would be better to go on to Camp Sherman and be ready to try for the horses later. By traveling through the remainder of the night and morning, they could reach the military camp before the stage arrived.

All Doyle and the others knew was the Apaches seemed to have left as silently as they had come. But, for the remainder of the night they stirred uneasily until the first light of dawn and, after a hasty breakfast, they were on their uncertain way to Camp Sherman.

CHAPTER THREE  INDIANS AT CAMP SHERMAN

By moving constantly, the Warm Springs band reached a narrow ridge above Camp Sherman shortly before noon and an hour ahead of the stage. The first thing they noticed was the camp was deserted. The corral was empty and no cooking fires were visible.

Nana pondered the turn of events. The soldiers' absence could mean only one thing – the uprising had spread to other sectors and the cavalry had been sent to intervene.

He also realized that their absence made his chances of stealing the horses a lot easier. The camp's corral was at least a hundred yards from the main camp and harder to guard than the one at the stage depot.

Situated as they were, they were unassailable. Inhabitants long before them had fortified the location, rendering it almost impregnable. Nana had often wondered about these strangers who had come and disappeared long before his time, or even within the memory of the eldest member of their band.

They had been Indian, of that he was certain. Flint chipings and arrowheads lay scattered about. The earlier ones had erected pit houses of some nature but not so different that the Apaches couldn't erect their wickiups on the exact sites where those dwellings once stood.

What had happened to them? *Had some enemy such as the whites invaded these lands and killed them all? Is this what is in store for all Indians?* The old man sighed in sorrow. The ways of Ussan were strange and hard to fathom.

He looked at the others, also resting after the long trek. Having few horses, they had been forced to trade off riding and walking. They were all brave young men who had grown tired of the humiliation and poisoned food their people were forced to endure. Yes, some would die, and, before it was over, he might be numbered among them. If such was the will of Ussan, when that day came it would be a good day to die.

The prospect of death – Indian attack, at the very least – lay heavy on the minds of the stage passengers despite the military escort. They had stopped three times during the course of the trip to Camp Sherman and each time the signs were unmistakably clear, the Apaches were somewhere ahead of them.

Their latest stop was just outside the entrance to Corduroy Canyon. And it was here that Butch, Doyle, and Whiting held a brief council while the passengers stretched their legs. All but the banker, who stayed inside the coach clutching his carpetbag and demanding that the stage leave at once.

Doyle eyed the canyon entrance just ahead. Once inside it, they exchanged the open prairie expanse for a narrow, twisting trail that lent itself to ambush almost every step of the way.

"Lieutenant, I've got a suggestion," Doyle said. "Butch says it's about another hour to Camp Sherman. We know the Apache are somewhere ahead of us and we also know they're few in number with little firepower, otherwise they would've done something before now."

He indicated the string of horses at the rear of the caravan. "Those animals are what they want but they aren't willing to sacrifice any lives to get them – at least so far. But, if they do intend to try and take them it's going to be sooner than later now that we're getting close to Camp Sherman."

"Go on," said Whiting.

"Then we need to make it as hard as possible on them. Let's put the horses in the middle and let the stage bring up the rear." He waved his hand, anticipating their response. "I know. I know. It's dusty as hell, but it won't be that long a ride."

Butch thought for a moment then said, "I believe it's a good idea, Marshal. The troopers can protect them a lot easier." He looked at Whiting. "As Chief Driver of North Star Stage Lines, I say we ought to do it, Lieutenant."

Doyle was satisfied with his strategy as they proceeded through the canyon. Each mile brought them closer to Camp Sherman and almost guaranteed safety. He saw no sign of Apaches, but that meant very little. If they didn't want to be seen, it was almost impossible to spot them until too late.

Inside the stage, Banker Wilson was his usual complaining self. Doyle almost spoke out once or twice, then thought better of it. All men like Wilson needed for someone to react to their whining. The others remained silent, their eyes glued to the walls of the canyon for any trace of an attack. Even Billy Joe managed to keep his mouth shut for a change.

"Camp Sherman just ahead!" Jeff leaned down from his shotgun position and shouted through the window.

"It's about time," said Wilson.

Doyle looked at the banker and Zacharias. They hadn't exchanged more than a few words the whole trip. They acted more like casual acquaintances than employer and employee and not even friendly acquaintances at that.

Lilly was the first to notice something was wrong. She was looking out the window when she realized there weren't any soldiers or horses visible. And there was no activity anywhere.

"Marshal Doyle," she said, "I don't think anyone's here."

Before Doyle could react to her remark the stage shuddered to a stop. A moment later he heard Butch's voice. "Marshal, you'd best step out and have a look!"

The stage had stopped in front of the camp commissary. Doyle could see that it was empty. He looked about, saw no one.

Lieutenant Whiting dismounted and immediately posted troopers as lookouts and went into the commissary. There he found a knife pinning a note to the bench from which the men ate. The note was from Corporal Keltze whom Whiting had left in charge.

It read: "Lt. Whiting, Dispatch arrived today ordering us to proceed with every man to Mogollon to assist in defense of expected Indian attack. Troops on patrol to reinforce Camp Vincent." The date on the note was July 6th.

When Whiting read the note to the little group, Banker Wilson was outraged and chastised Lieutenant Whiting, "The army has deserted its post and left innocent civilians to the mercy of the savage Apache."

Whiting responded, "It is the army's duty to protect all, not just one person. We'll be all right and get through."

These words of assurance did little to placate Banker Wilson and he left the commissary tent muttering audibly, "Only damn fools join the army."

Whiting gave orders, "Look to your weapons and be ready to move out under cover of darkness." The horses were placed in the rock corrals directly across the canyon from the commissary tent. There was a good store of native grass which the soldiers had cut with scythes and piled in a little shed alongside the corrals. Whiting ordered that the horses be given extra rations and that the passengers would rest and then they'd leave at midnight.

It would be dark and difficult traveling but the road stayed in the canyon bottom for several miles and, with the exception of crossing the marshes of Corduroy Lake, there were no hazards to face other than the prospect of an Indian attack.

Marshal Doyle had unshackled his prisoner, Billy Joe, freeing his hands and his legs so he could help the soldiers feed the horses and also assist tightening and greasing the wheels of the stage.

A half hour before sunset, the Marshal called the prisoner over to the commissary tent and started to reshackle and handcuff him. Billy Joe pled, "For Gods sake let me protect myself."

The Marshal thought, It isn't fair to keep him in handcuffs and leg irons if an attack does take place so he handcuffed his hands and left the shackles off his legs.

Marshal Doyle was a tough, taciturn, and dedicated peace officer, but he was also a man of considerable compassion and took no joy in hauling this young man off to trial and possible execution. He knew that the Western system of justice was harsh and severe and that the punishment meted out for many crimes was disproportionate to the offense.

The Marshal was looking at the tail end of a career going downhill. The Magdalena assignment was a substantial step backward for the Marshal who had been U.S. Marshal for the Territory of Oklahoma before he got in trouble after a prisoner escaped his custody.

Prisoners captured in the Oklahoma Territory were taken to Fort Smith, Arkansas, for trial. The last overnight stop before reaching Fort Smith was Whitefield, Oklahoma. At Whitefield, Oklahoma, there was a small ranching and farming community and a giant oak tree in the center of town which took on the function of a jail whenever prisoners were spending the night in Whitefield. Since there was no secure building or jail in the community which could house the prisoners, they were cuffed hand-to-hand around the giant oak.

Sometimes as many as two or three wagonloads amounting to thirty prisoners would be connected together in this fashion and, while it wasn't the most comfortable of accommodations for the prisoners, it nevertheless was quite effective and no one had ever been able to escape from the oak tree. That is until the evening of January 3, 1874, when Marshal Doyle, with two wagonloads of prisoners arrived in Whitefield at sundown.

The prisoners were allowed to relieve themselves one or two at a time under the watchful eyes of the guards. Then a dinner was prepared for them around an open campfire. The last operation to secure the prisoners for night was to pass a long chain around the tree going through the handcuffed arms of each prisoner. The chain was then padlocked and a more secure, escape-proof prison could not be imagined.

That night, after the prisoners had been fed and bedded down, Marshal Doyle stepped across the street to the home of Dr. James Culbertson, an old friend of his. Dr. Culbertson was the only doctor in the area and, in order to feed his family, also operated the ferry across the Canadian River. The Doc and Marshal Doyle had been friends for many years and always had a drink or two together whenever Marshal Doyle came through Whitefield. This particular night they had a friendly visit and, after a couple of drinks, Marshal Doyle was getting ready to go back to the encampment to spend the night when three shots were heard across the river.

Dr. Culbertson looked up and said, "Wouldn't you know it, the minute I'm ready to call it quits for the night, there is always someone over there wanting to come across. Well this night he can just stay. Whoever it is, I'll be danged if I'm gonna take the time to go get some drunk cowboy safely across the Canadian River."

Fanny Culbertson, the doctor's wife, overheard his complaint and promptly chastised him: "Dr. James, you know Rowland's still out," referring to their oldest son, "and I don't want him spending the night across the Canadian. I worry too much as it is. You go get that cowboy, whoever it is."

Marshal Doyle allowed, "I'll go with you Doc, I've got plenty of time and would enjoy letting you give me a ride across the river."

The two men left the house and walked a few yards down the river bank and got on the ferry which was a raft that ran on pulleys connected to a wire cable that crossed the Canadian. The span at this point was about a hundred yards. The ferry was moved both by poles and pulling on one loop of the cable.

Ten minutes later they were on the north bank. Sitting on a stump holding the reins of his horse was the missing Roland. The doctor exclaimed, "Roland, I've told you time and again to get back before dark. The next time you can cool your heels over here all night." Roland, sheepishly offered no defense but took the berating as just punishment for staying out so late and inconveniencing his father. The only other option would have been a very dangerous nighttime swim in a river filled with shifting sandbars and quicksand.

When they reached the other side, Marshal Doyle said goodnight to his friend and cautioned young Roland to start carrying a timepiece so he wouldn't be late again. The Marshal quickly strode back to the camp, saw that his men were all sound asleep and, before turning in himself, decided to check the prisoners.

To his despair and amazement no men were around the tree. All that was left was the chain that had been used to tie them together. The Marshal quickly woke his deputies and they hastily determined that none of the prisoners were still in camp. The Marshal then inspected the chain and saw that the lock was still on, but another length of chain about six feet long was attached by the lock to the official chain the Marshal had meant to tie the prisoner with. It became obvious that someone had cleverly slipped a false chain into the chaining process and this short, unattached piece had been used to form the final link with the padlock.

The Marshal's speculation was correct. One of the prisoners, Whitie Leslie, had been to Fort Smith by prison wagon a couple of years before and, when he found out that's where he was heading again, he managed to get word to a friend who supplied him with a section of chain. The night before they had stopped in the community of Weeletka and the wagons had been taken to the livery to be greased. While they were being greased, Whitie's friend hid the length of chain under some straw in a corner of the wagon that Whitie was riding in. Whitie had concealed the chain by wrapping it around his body and successfully had evaded discovery by the guards. That night when it came time to chain up, Whitie took a position closest to the campfire because he knew that's where the guards would start with their chain and also finish. Whitie had been right and very lucky and he was the last man before the chain was secured.

The prisoners were required to pass the chain from prisoner to prisoner while a guard looked on to make sure it passed through their hands. Whitie, who was one of the pioneer safe-crackers of the West, deftly managed to substitute his chain for the real chain in making the final connection. Grasping both the prison chain and his chain in his right hand so as to make it appear that they were one and the same. The ruse worked and the deception went undetected. As a result, the prisoners were free to pass the loose chain between them and effect an escape to the last man once the guards had turned in for the night.

The anger of the Marshal was only matched by his embarrassment and well he knew that his skin was on the line with this kind of failure.

A search was mounted that night and eight of the escapees were found hiding in various places in town including wood piles, the livery stables, and one on Doc Culbertson's ferry under some burlap bags. The next day, the search went on and by noon only five prisoners were unaccounted for, one of which was Whitie Leslie. Marshal Doyle chained the prisoners for the night and early next morning started for Fort Smith and his own judgment.

Whitie made good on his escape and three months later was seen by a friend in El Paso, Texas boarding the Butterfield Stage for California. He was never seen in the Southwest again. The reason Whitie had made good on his escape from Whitefield was because he took the one escape route that everyone knew was impossible. Whitie swam the Canadian River at night handcuffed by heavy manacles. He had done it by finding a log and using it as a raft to keep his upper body afloat while he kicked with his legs. This crude arrangement worked and carried him downstream almost six miles before he could reach the other side. The drifting downstream worked to his advantage by giving him an additional lead.

After reaching Fort Smith, there was a good chance that the Marshal might lose his federal commission but, fortunately, he had friends in the service who realized how terrible being cashiered would be to the self-respect and dignity of this good man. Instead, he was banished to the hinterlands and had suffered at his post in Magdalena for a full two years.

Young Billy Joe took the first chance he saw to escape custody. When the Marshal was outside the commissary handing a box of supplies to Butch to lash to the top of the stage, Billy Joe slipped under the back wall of the commissary tent and quickly moved into the adjacent tree line. He rapidly slipped from tree to tree, distancing himself from the camp.

He now had to decide which way to make his escape and, since he had never been in this part of the country before, he had to act on pure instinct. He reasoned, *If I go up or down the canyon then they will track me and overtake me on horseback. If I make for the high country and the rocks, it will be difficult to trail me or maneuver a horse in pursuit.* He moved quickly along the rocky ridge that headed due south from Camp Sherman, gaining altitude in the fading light.

He was panting and out of breath. He was not moving with stealth but was hurrying to get as far from the Marshal's grasp as quickly as he could. He was traveling along an old trail which led to a large rock next to a fallen tree. Here the trail topped out and he stopped for a moment, sitting on the rock to regain his breath. As he did, he thought about his predicament and realized, for the first time, that he had not taken any food.

Well, so be it, he thought. As a youngster he had caught many a rabbit for the family pot using snares and, if need be, he could live off the wild berries, grapes, and tubers of the region long enough to perfect his escape. As Billy Joe got up to move on, he noticed there was a second ridge leading off to the right of the ridge he was on that, after a small swale, narrowed down into a very narrow crest. Obviously, a horse could not cross this kind of barrier in the night. Without hesitation, he diverted to the right and crossed the swale and started climbing the ridge. The jumble of rocks was so interwoven that he had to actually lift himself up with his hands from rock to rock as he negotiated his way along the spine. There was no way that he could have known that he was climbing right into the middle of the hidden Warm Springs Apache raiders, and that his next step would bring him face to face with Tis-ta-dae.

After killing Billy Joe, Tis-ta-dae waited for a moment to be sure no one else was coming along the trail and then hurried back to the small group. At the second line of breastworks he met his friend Chubasco coming up to join him and hurriedly told him what had happened. Chubasco went back for help while Tis-ta-dae returned to the scene of the encounter.

It wasn't long before the entire band had reached Tis-ta-dae's position. Three of the braves lifted the body up over the rocks and onto a little clearing in back of the breastworks. They examined the arrow which had transfixed the body with such force. No one had ever seen an arrow so deeply embedded before. They marveled at the strength of Tis-ta-dae. In the fading light they examined the bow. It was one that Tis-ta-dae had made himself under his grandfather's supervision. It was the typical Apache bow made from native mulberry with a reverse curve in the manner of the Turkish bow. Like many Apache bows, it had been reinforced with an applique of sinew on its backside. To fix the applique required great dexterity, patience, and many hours of work. But it was well worth the effort and it gave the bow the strength and spring of one twice its length.

The point that Tis-ta-dae had put on the arrow was obsidian. It was a point he had found in the ruins of a Mogollon Pueblo on Diamond Creek. It was the most beautiful point he had ever seen, finely worked and razor sharp.

As soon as the excitement had subsided, Nana determined that they should immediately move to take the horses. He knew from the fact the young man was in handcuffs that he was a prisoner of some kind and must have escaped. In the confusion that might follow, perhaps they could seize the opportunity to run off the remuda. He quickly outlined a plan of assault, "Chubasco, you pick three men and charge the Camp. Don't overrun it, just draw their fire and keep them busy while the rest of us run off the horses."

CHAPTER FOUR

CAPTURE THE REMUDA

The Apaches moved down the old trail which more than a thousand years earlier had provided the pit dwellers of the ridge access to Corduroy Lake and their fields of corn, squash, and beans. When they reached the bottom, the group split, half the besiegers went to the right towards the commissary tent, and the rest stayed on the left side of the canyon and moved up to the corral.

The corral was made of unmortared rock on three sides and built against a vertical cliff thirty feet high. The corral crossed a stream that ran down the canyon to Corduroy Lake and provided an excellent enclosure for the horses. There was a small shed on the eastern side of the corral where hay and cavalry gear was kept. There were two troopers on guard at this shed. They heard the sound of the rock wall being torn down, and called the alarm, "Apaches! Apaches!" while rushing to defend their outpost.

A fusillade of arrows met the onrushing guards. The soldiers responded with rapid fire from their carbines. In less than ten seconds, three Indians were down and both troopers were on the ground, one dead and the other badly wounded. One Indian was dead; two were wounded. One of them was Tis-ta-dae who took a forty caliber slug in the thigh, just barely missing the femur while tearing out a large chunk of flesh. The other wound was to the right side of his face. A bullet had creased the jaw, breaking it and tearing off half of the right ear.

The whites were pinned down in the commissary tent, not knowing the attack on them was only a diversion. They could hear the rapid fire and whoops coming from the corrals but didn't dare leave the security of their position to aid the soldiers guarding the horses.

The second it was obvious that both positions were under attack, Whiting realized that he had blundered. He had wanted to concentrate everyone at the corrals until it was time to leave but Banker Wilson had raised hell about having to spend time in a "filthy stable." Against his better judgment, the Lieutenant split the party and now was paying the price with the corral defenders out of action and the commissary position in peril.

The Indians could easily have pressed their attack on the commissary but this was not their goal. They had come after horses and now they had them. Excitedly, in the fading moonlight, they headed the horses towards Doggie Canyon. The besiegers of the commissary broke off the engagement and joined their friends, helping drive the horses. They reached Doggie Canyon and turned right heading towards their principal Warm Springs Village, Ojos Caliente.

Marshal Doyle had missed the attack, having gone up the canyon trying to find the trail of his prisoner. When the shooting commenced, he hurried back towards the camp and was right in the path of the fleeing Indians. He hid behind a group of rocks that jutted out into the canyon and fired at the Indians as they passed. He did not know it, but he hit one of the warriors who later died.

Doyle continued down to the camp and called out, "It's me, Doyle. Don't shoot." He told the excited defenders, "The Indians have vamoosed with the horses and are long gone."

Whiting reconnoitered the corral with the remaining troopers and found the wounded man and the dead soldier.

They were brought back to the commissary tent and the group spent a restless night waiting for the dawn with Lil administering to the wounded soldier and Zacharias Smith throughout the night. The soldier had been hit with six arrows. One had penetrated the abdomen and presented the most serious threat. Zacharias had been hit in the head by a bullet and was dead by morning.

At dawn they assessed their damages. The horses were gone except for one of the stagecoach animals and two cavalry mounts which were grazing up the canyon along the little stream. They had split from the bunch that the Indians had run off during the night. Whiting, Butch, and Jeff Bartlett retrieved the horses after a short chase and brought them in. The problem now was how to proceed with two horses who had never been hitched to a stage and were undoubtedly going to raise hell.

Butch Garrison had faced a similar situation once and had

solved it by blindfolding the horses, putting them in hitch, and then keeping their saddles on, having a rider mount each giving the horse a feeling of security and assurance.

It took a while to rework the harness so the lead horse was pulling from a single tree and was hitched in front of the draw bar which had been cut off at midpoint. Whiting and Sergeant Baskind mounted the cavalry horses and their blindfolds were removed. Amazingly, the horses did not bolt, they were nervous and wild-eyed but they remained under control and the stage pulled out from Camp Sherman and rattled down the canyon across the corduroy log road over the marshy land skirting the lake.

The dead trooper and Zacharias Smith had been placed in the boot. Six miles down the twisting canyon, the stage broke out onto Corduroy Flats, a large flat area devoid of trees and knee high in black Gramma grass. It stretched for three miles to the southeast and was over a mile wide. Coming in from the right was Spring Canyon and there was located the mailbox tree. The stage left the stage road for a half a mile to reach the tree to see if there were any messages there. There were none, Butch directed Jeff, "Don't leave the gun and ammo here, we may need them before we get to Silver."

They took time here to bury the trooper and Smith in shallow graves, erecting rock cairns to prevent the bodies being dug up by wolves. By this time, the wounded man, Trooper Ron Jackson, had weakened and was running a high fever. Lillian continued to administer to him, keeping his forehead cool and moist with a dampened handkerchief and assuring him, "You'll be ok, I won't leave you for a minute."

None of the men shared Lilly's optimism. They all knew how serious a gut wound was and what little prospect there would be for a recovery once peritonitis set in. To them, a wound in the gut was the same as rabies. Rabies, maybe, was even the better of the two because it was over sooner.

It was now the middle of their third day out and they were half way toward Silver City but smack in the heart of the most unpopulated area of the United States. Strangely enough, a thousand years earlier this area had teamed with villages of Mogollon Pueblo Indians.

Literally thousands of Indians had lived in the Gila Basin in large villages, some of two hundred houses and more. These Indians had extensive fields and developed one of the finest pottery styles in all the new world. Mimbres pottery was highly sought by all of the adjacent Pueblo tribes as the finest development of the potter's art. Mysteriously, about 1150 A.D., they had disappeared totally from the Gila area and there was little or no Indian occupation of the mountains of the Southwest until the Athabaskan Apache groups began to arrive just ahead of the Spaniards.

The stage road pulled out of Corduroy Flats up a fairly steep incline which was too much for three horses. By now the cavalry mounts had become resigned to their new fate as draft animals and were pulling like regular hands. Everyone except Lilly, the wounded man and Butch, had to dismount and assist by turning the wheels by hand to keep their upward movement going.

They topped out and began a long descent along Cemetery Ridge to Camp Vincent. They reached the camp located at the junction of Taylor Creek and Beaver Creek, the start of the east fork of the Gila River. The camp, like Sherman, was totally deserted, only here there were no messages to enlighten them. It was obvious something had happened on sudden notice as the commissary had plenty of food and there were even boxes of ammunition in the quartermaster's stores.

Without wasting time, Whiting put the extra ammunition on board the stage. They turned around and followed Taylor Creek upstream to its junction with Hoyt Creek, then they followed it upward until they crossed over and dropped into Diamond Creek.

The stream was flowing briskly and they stopped to rest their animals. Whiting climbed up on a low mesa which projected into the valley where there was a good view both up and down Diamond Creek. He stood on a mound which was part of the debris from a large Mogollon village which had once occupied this site. Scattered about were broken pieces of pottery, metates, and other refuse of the centuries of occupation the site had seen.

Everything was quiet. There was no smoke in sight. Nothing to warn you that death lurked in that beautiful view of sky, trees, and mountains. Whiting clambered back down the old Indian trail to the valley floor, ordered the stage forward. Jackson was becoming delirious, yelling for water. Lil patiently bathed his forehead and spoke softly to him, telling him that he would see a doctor soon.

"Hold on! Be brave!" she told him.

As Banker Wilson watched this beautiful lady give her heart and soul to the wounded man, he felt shame and, for the first time in his life, despised his own standards. He thought to himself, *If we come through this mess, somehow I'll make it up to this courageous lady I have wronged.*

Banker Wilson had come through all of the perilous adventures of the last few days without ever once letting go of his carpetbag. It was with him constantly. He used it as a pillow. It was next to him on the seat or under his feet on the floorboards. It was his shield in the battle of the commissary tent. Never was it out of sight. Several times, the Marshal had wondered what Wilson had in the valise, but too many things were happening too fast to ask those kinds of questions.

About three miles up Diamond Creek, the trail left the bottom and veered back to the south beginning a gentle ascent to the top of an escarpment that looked down upon Black Canyon. Here, the passengers got out to lighten the load. Not so the horses could pull up a hill but so that the brakes would not fail on the way down. Only Lilly and the wounded man stayed in the coach as it began the perilous creaking descent into Black Canyon.

When they reached the bottom of Black Canyon, they stopped to rest the horses and get ready for the next climb upward and then the torturous negotiation of Rocky Canyon. It was almost dark and they made camp by the side of the small stream in the canyon bottom. Here Whiting cached some of the ammunition in order to lighten the load for the climb out of the canyon in the morning. Driver Butch found time to do a little fishing and caught enough native Gila trout for a good hot dinner for all, cooked on a small fire shielded on all sides by large boulders.

Trooper Jackson spent a restless night, often crying out. Lilly had made a pallet along side of him and would put her hand over his mouth whenever he cried out in pain. His body was raging with fever and his speech was incoherent. The next morning, they hurriedly put their gear back on the stage and once again departed.

This pull was even harder than the other and, on several occasions, it seemed they wouldn't make it. The cavalry horses were just not bred for this kind of hard work. But with the shouting of Butch and the sweat and toil of everyone they finally pulled out on top and dropped into Rocky Canyon.

Rocky Canyon was aptly named. It was not a long part of the journey but it was the slowest part. It was a short deep canyon that connected two ridges and had to be traversed in order to gain the better ground along the ridge lines. Right in the middle of Rocky Canyon the road was so strewn with boulders that the wheels had to be hand manipulated to get them over. In one particularly narrow place, where the stage had to turn abruptly right in order to get through, the rear wheels began to slip.

It looked for a moment like the stage was going to overturn. Whiting and Doyle were on the left side and, at great personal risk, planted their shoulders on the side of the stage and let their bodies serve as a brace to keep it from tipping. Meanwhile Butch cajoled the horses and manipulated the reigns while the others turned the wheels by hand and got the stage through.

CHAPTER FIVE  TIS-TA-DAE'S ORDEAL

Rain began to fall gently across the Gila as the small band of Warm Springs Apache made their way eastward with the remuda of horses they had just stolen from the corrals at Camp Sherman. Tis-ta-dae's heart was full of pride for the Apaches, considering that this small group had successfully stolen some thirty horses from the United States Cavalry. His pride was undiminished by the severe wounds he had received in breaching the corral at Camp Sherman and overcoming the Cavalry guards.

Tis-ta-dae, despite his wounds, had caught one of the horses and joined in pushing the remuda up Corduroy Canyon. He had been able to stay mounted and keep up with the band for the first hour after the engagement but now he was getting weaker from loss of blood and the pain was beginning to shoot through his whole body.

The wound in Tis-ta-dae's jaw would affect him the rest of his life. It was the wound in the thigh, however, which was causing immediate distress. The bullet had entered from the right-hand side of the thigh and passed completely through, tearing out a hunk of flesh the size of a fist. The older warriors had stuffed the wound with dried grass at their first stop an hour after the attack and had bound it with Tis-ta-dae's shirt but it was still bleeding badly.

Nana was very concerned about Tis-ta-dae's condition. Near midnight, he halted the little band on a sloping ridge and personally examined Tis-ta-dae's wounds. He didn't like what he saw. The wound in the leg was still bleeding and blood was running down Tis-ta-dae's leg.

Nana suggested that Tis-ta-dae stay behind and that they send a party back for him with a travois. Tis-ta-dae, by motions, insisted that he could make it. He was determined to enter the Warm Springs camp in triumph with the rest of the raiders.

An hour later, Nana was getting ready to call a halt in order to check on Tis-ta-dae again when he saw that Tis-ta-dae had slumped forward and was slipping from his horse. Before Nana could help Tis-ta-dae, he had fallen from the animal and was laying on the ground on his right side. The fall had knocked the leg bindings loose, and the wound was hemorrhaging.

Nana quickly removed the dressing and stuffed new grass into the wound to create pressure and stop the bleeding. Again the wound was bound but by this time Tis-ta-dae was unconscious. It was obvious that he couldn't go on and, in fact, the consensus was that he would be dead by morning anyway. With regret, Nana made the decision to leave Tis-ta-dae there and hurry on toward camp. Nana was very nervous. He knew that the cavalry, if they received reinforcements, would be hot on their trail and that they would not tolerate the theft of such a valuable commodity as a remuda of horses. The ridge where Nana left Tis-ta-dae was about ten miles from Camp Sherman and they had another twenty miles to travel to reach Ojos Caliente.

Dawn was breaking in the east when Nana and the warriors arrived at the main Warm Springs Camp at Ojo Caliente. There was great excitement with the announcement of the camp dogs that one of the war parties was returning. Every man, woman, and child turned out to greet the victorious warriors and admire their prize. The great council drum was brought out and two of the braves began to beat out the solemn cadence of the war dance while singing with great gusto, "Hey-ya-ney Hey-ya-ney ney-ney Hey-ya-ney."

The returning braves and then other adults and finally the children begin to move their feet and shuffle to the rhythm of the drum. This was a mighty victory to celebrate and no one could belittle the importance of the capture of so many fine animals. Four parties had been sent out looking for horses. Two returned ahead of Nana. One empty handed and the other with six animals.

At this point in the celebration, the fourth party made its appearance and, fortunately, it brought twenty-five captive horses with it. This party had been down on the Rio Grande working amongst the homesteads seeking additional animals. They reported that there had been three brushes with farmers and two whites had been killed. The joy of the celebration was cooled somewhat as everyone realized that with deaths occurring among the whites in two of the raids, retribution might follow swiftly. On the other hand, the war council, five nights earlier, had considered all these consequences and made the fateful decision to seek horses and actively prosecute a fight for independence from the spreading cancer of white domination.

It was almost midmorning when Nana, flushed with excitement, remembered that he had not sent anyone back to bring in the body of Tis-ta-dae. He asked two of the younger braves to take a horse and return for Tis-ta-dae's body. After all, Tis-ta-dae had been a brave warrior. He had killed the first white and had been on the point when the horses were captured. He had conducted himself as would a warrior of many years and earned the respect and admiration of everyone in the small group of raiders.

Tis-ta-dae's family did not take part in the celebration and stayed in their wickiups lamenting the death of Tis-ta-dae. If ever a young Apache boy had been marked for a great leadership role, it was Tis-ta-dae, they all agreed. After all, as a boy of fourteen, he and one of the De la O' boys from Monticello had lured a great grizzly bear to its death. And here on this successful trip, he had killed one of the whites, passing an arrow completely through his body – to the marvel of everyone else on the expedition.

Everyone had counted on Tis-ta-dae's returning and knew that only he, by his cheerful presence, could give his mother the strength to recover from a rattlesnake bite that she had received three days earlier. It was a small snake, typical of the Green Rock Rattlers of the Black Range and Gila, but deadly enough that Tis-ta-dae's mother was in great danger. Her right leg was swollen to the hip and there was an ominous sign of blood poisoning in the fiery red vein that coursed up her thigh.

She was so feverish that she had to be restrained to prevent her hurting herself in her delusions. She had not been told that Tis-ta-dae had been mortally wounded on the raid. Instead they told her that he was on his way in and had been left behind by the others so that he could rest and keep from aggravating his honorable battle wounds.

But Tis-ta-dae was far from dead and his miraculous survival is perpetuated among the remnants of the Warm Springs Apache as truly one of the great manifestations of the special status of the Warm Springs.

Tis-ta-dae had wakened in the morning after being left behind, feeling the rain falling cold on his forehead and hearing a rasping sound. He felt something warm stroking the wound on his leg. The bandage had been loosened baring the wound, and a lobo wolf was cleaning and dressing the wound with its warm tongue.

He slowly opened his eyes and raised his head enough to see the wolf busy at his chores. The young boy was terrified. While the wolf was only half grown, it still weighed at least fifty pounds and could have torn him to pieces if it wanted. He had seen wolves before in the wild but never one this close. The thought occurred to Tis-ta-dae that this was just a dream but if he was dead, why did he hurt so much, not only his leg, but the whole right side of his head where the jaw had been broken by a grazing bullet leaving a furrow in the flesh four inches long and baring the bone throughout its course. In addition, the lower half of his right ear had been torn off by the bullet.

Convinced by the throbbing pain that he really wasn't dead, Tis-ta-dae began to appreciate his predicament. By this time, the wolf had laid down beside him. Dare Tis-ta-dae disturb this animal and start to make his way to the Warm Springs Camp or should he stay perfectly still until the wolf left?

With strength beginning to return to his body and the fever abating, he decided to attempt to join his family and comrades. First he reached down with his right hand and stroked the wolf's tail. The wolf raised its head and turned to face the boy. Tis-ta-dae's heart skipped a beat as the wolf looked at him with baleful eyes and then it began to whimper softly in sympathy with the boy.

Tis-ta-dae, with difficulty, got to his feet. He was limping badly as he searched for a stick with a fork in it that would be long enough for him to use as a crutch. He needed support for his right leg. The muscles had been so badly damaged, that he had no control. He finally found a piece of wood with a fork but it was too long and he had to break it to a suitable length using two large stones, one as a hammer, and the other as an anvil.

The effort brought searing pain to both his leg and his jaw but he had no recourse. He had to be on his way. The wolf watched Tis-ta-dae curiously and, obviously, wanted to be the boy's companion. When finally Tis-ta-dae had fashioned his crude crutch and begun to hobble towards the east, the wolf stood up and accompanied him walking alongside the boy's badly injured leg as if to protect it.

Tis-ta-dae, after packing the wound with fresh grass, hobbled along for three miles, gaining strength with each step of the way, his mind a torrent of thoughts. How quickly he had passed into manhood. Fresh from his initiation ceremonies on his first campaign as a warrior, killing one of the enemy in a face-to-face encounter, and now helped by a wolf brother to recover from the great wound to his leg.

So preoccupied was Tis-ta-dae with thoughts of his ordeal that at first he didn't hear the shout of greeting from two of his close friends riding together on a horse towards him across an open meadow.

"Tis-ta-dae, Tis-ta-dae," they shouted, "Tis-ta-dae, you're alive. Tis-ta-dae you're alive."

Recognizing the voices, Tis-ta-dae began to wave his arms, dropping the crutch, standing on one foot, overjoyed that his friends had sought him out. They were two boys his own age with whom he had grown up. One had been with him on the recent horse raiding expedition. Tis-ta-dae's friends spurred the horse to a gallop and, when half way across the meadow, still shouting and waving, they spied the lobo wolf at Tis-ta-dae's side. They reigned the horse up, not knowing what to make of this strange combination of a boy and a wolf pup. The wolf was puzzled even more than they. It had never seen a horse before and all this shouting and noise was strange and confusing. It acted instinctively, and wheeled and ran toward the tree line, never looking back, forgetting the bond it had formed with this creature that had been hurt and possessed such strange fascination for the young wolf.

Tis-ta-dae's friends again rushed forward with the departure of the wolf and, on reaching Tis-ta-dae, smothered him with embraces and questions and shouts of exaltation, "You're alive! How wonderful, you're alive!"

The friends continued to embrace Tis-ta-dae and praise his recovery. They shouted their happiness to see him alive and their amazement that he was with the wolf, calling him, "Tis-ta-dae Wolf Brother."

The questions poured in on Tis-ta-dae but he could not answer. His jaw was totally immobilized from his wound and broken in three places. By signs, however, he indicated that he was okay and glad to see them and that the wolf was indeed his brother. He signed that the wolf had licked his wounds and purified it and made it clean and free from infection. The two boys carefully helped Tis-ta-dae mount the horse and then, leading it, took off at a fast walk across Burnt Cabin Flat, heading towards Ojos Caliente to spread the amazing news of Tis-ta-dae's survival.

It was near dark when the three boys and the tired mount reached the main Warm Springs encampment. Shouts of joy greeted the appearance of Tis-ta-dae, whom everyone had assumed was dead. Happiest of all was Nana who in celebration vowed to himself to place a small cache of sacred tobacco in a crevice of a rock where Nana went often to seek comfort and solace.

By now Tis-ta-dae was much recovered and able to sign vigorously what had happened to him. He attempted to speak from time to time, forgetting his wound, but was prevented from doing so by the broken jaw and terrible pain the exertion provoked. Tis-ta-dae asked to see his mother as soon as possible. They led him off to the wickiup where she lay dying. When he entered, he could smell the corruption of the flesh and could see in her eyes the despair of a dying woman.

Then – a flicker of joy – as she recognized her son, and cried out, "Tis-ta-dae, Tis-ta-dae, come to me my son."

He knelt over his mother, embracing her, tears flowing freely. His long black hair cascading over her head and shoulders. Mother and son in that sorrowful but exalted moment communicated to each other by touch and force of mind the great love and respect they had for each other. Then with a convulsion, the woman died.

Tis-ta-dae clung to the lifeless body for a minute, finally struggling upright, seeing the horribly distended leg where the rattlesnake had placed its poison, puffed and black, presaging the death that came so swiftly.

Tis-ta-dae could not stay in the wickiup of his mother where women would spend the rest of the night preparing her for the ceremony leading to her interment. Instead, Nana led him off to his own wickiup where he administered to the wounds. He applied a compress of Yerba Buena to the wound on the leg, marveling that there was no infection.

"How clean it is," he said, "already healing."

He had never heard of a wolf doing such a thing and yet he well knew that throughout the animal world this was the manner in which wounds were treated. He saw that the jaw was going to be the real problem for Tis-ta-dae. He knew that it had to be immobilized, and yet Tis-ta-dae had to receive nourishment.

Nana worked long into the night with help from Lozen, a medicine woman, fashioning a splint for the outside of the jaw, which consisted of two pieces of wood. One was short and under the jaw. The other was longer and placed to the side. These were held together by a hinge of sinew passing through holes he had drilled with a stone awl lashed to a section of reed. This was then supported by bandages wrapped around the head, effectively holding the jaw in place. The teeth did not close in a normal fashion for Nana had placed a tapered wooden bridge between the top and bottom teeth, which caused the front of the jaws to remain open about a quarter of an inch. This same wedge was placed on the left side to keep the jaw aligned during the healing process. The bridge was to hold the jaw slightly open so that liquid nourishment could be administered.

With the jaw broken in three places and the tissue swollen and distended, the placing of the splint produced excruciating pain. No one, however, was surprised that Tis-ta-dae did not call out, for there was no one in that camp who would have displayed human frailty under a similar circumstance. Nana's medical expertise was effective. Not only would the jaw heal, but it would leave Tis-ta-dae with little functional disability. His speech would be totally unaffected.

The jaw, when fully healed, would give Tis-ta-dae a fierce appearance. The deep furrow would remain forever and provoke discussion about Tis-ta-dae's amazing experience with the wolf.

The next morning when Tis-ta-dae awakened, he expected to see Nana by his side but he was not there. Later, when Lozen came to feed him a gruel made from oat mast and venison broth, he indicated by signs that he wanted to speak with Nana and was told that Nana had left the camp with thirty warriors to join the Mimbreno band to capture more horses.

Tis-ta-dae was disappointed that Nana had gone off on a campaign leaving him behind but there was no doubt he was going to be unfit for the life of a warrior for months so he busied himself helping prepare the camp for what was to come. It was obvious that the Americans who had settled them within the confines of a small reservation would be forcing their removal as the miners and trappers and settlers had for so long been demanding.

Knowing this, about half the tribe packed their gear and belongings and began to slip away to the rugged wilderness area surrounding the middle and western forks of the Gila River. Here, at least, there were, as yet, no white settlers, encroachments, or mining prospects.

With his mother dead, Tis-ta-dae joined one of these groups despite his wounds and it was with great sadness that Tis-ta-dae looked back and said good bye to the Warm Springs Camp at Ojos Caliente.

CHAPTER SIX  NORTH STAR MESA

The beleaguered party left Rocky Canyon behind and reached the top of the next ridge. Directly ahead of them lay North Star Mesa, where the road ran straight for twenty miles with hardly a bump or shimmy to disturb the ride. They spent the night here in a dry camp. Everyone shared their canteen water with Lilly so she could continue to bathe the wounded trooper. He was less agitated now. No longer calling out, only uttering low pitiful moans, his body racked with pain.

About an hour after sunset, the moon began to rise and, mercifully, Trooper Jackson drifted into a comatose state. Whiting, seeing the trooper was quiet, insisted that Lilly leave him for a while and take some rest from her constant nursing.

There was a formation of low lying ledge rocks about fifty feet from the where they were camped and Whiting walked there with Lilly and told the sentry he had posted, "Take a break, I'll stand your post."

The Lieutenant and the woman who had been run out of town spent a short time together, each afraid to say a word to the other about his and her personal interest. The Lieutenant, because of the tenseness of the moment and responsibility that was his to see this party through, could not afford to play the part of a moonstruck young lover and be derelict in his duty. Lilly could not lead the Lieutenant on without being honest and truthful. She felt unworthy of his attention and ashamed of her own life.

The Lieutenant constantly surveyed the terrain, listening for any unusual sound. Lilly's eyes and thoughts were only on Whiting. The guard returned and they walked back to the stage and the sleeping figures around it. Holding hands was as intimate as they became. To Lilly that was enough.

In the morning they were up early, a cold breakfast and on the road. The fifth day had begun and it was to be downhill all the way now. They were out of the rugged Gila Basin. They were nearing Silver City and the large cavalry post at Fort Bayard.

The three horses were pulling together smoothly and the road was gentle. Trooper Jackson was near death. But still, Lilly kept him as comfortable as she could, cooling his forehead with her wet handkerchief. By noon they had reached that point on the trail where the North Star Mesa began to drop toward Sapillo Creek. Butch brought the horses to a faster trot and the tempo of the trip quickened.

Then, it happened. To the right side of the stage at the edge of the tree line, a hundred yards away, appeared a band of thirty mounted Apaches riding parallel to the stage, brandishing their weapons. The lead rider, dressed in leggings and loin cloth, stripped to the waist, and painted for war, was old man Nana himself.

Nana debated giving the order to charge the stage which he knew was the same one they had previously harassed. He wanted to obtain more horses and he was sorely short of guns. Against the cavalry, lances and bows and arrows just were not enough. There were guns aboard that stage he knew and he also knew that the occupants had been worn down by the fight at Camp Sherman. He, himself, had seen the two troopers prone on the ground in the corrals, and Tis-ta-dae had killed a young man on the ridge. If anyone else had been disabled, there would be very little response from the stage, so he gave the signal by lowering his lance to the left and crying out to the braves, "Attack!"

The attack began, swinging a quarter to the left at a full gallop, bearing down on the stage.

Butch took his whip and popped it on the horses' backs and yelled and cursed, while Bartlett threw rocks at the horses to quicken their pace. He then turned and began firing his forty caliber carbine at the approaching line of hostiles.

Banker Wilson, for the first time that anyone had seen on the trip, opened his valise and reached inside and pulled out a pistol and, reaching through the window, began to fire at the Indians. Marshal Doyle had done the same. And Whiting who had been riding on top, stretched flat on the roof of the stage and began to fire with great effect. One, two, and then three of the Indians fell from their mounts in this withering fire.

The Indians were too far away to be effective with their primitive weapons. Still they came, closer and closer, their horses nostrils flared, straining every sinew under the demand of their riders, until finally arrows were becoming effective. The first person hit was Banker Wilson, who took an arrow in the flesh of his left shoulder. Then the Marshal caught an arrow in his left arm. It was not disabling, however, and he continued to pour steady fire out the window of the stage.

Closer the Indians came, they were surrounding the stage, and about to envelope the jaded and slowing animals, when the stage reached the end of the straight run of North Star Mesa and turned abruptly to the right to begin its descent to the Sapillo.

At this point, by fortunate coincidence, a large group of miners were camped, resting their animals after having pulled out of the valley.

The stage thundered through the miners' camp, along with most of the Indians. A wild melee ensued. The miners, at first confused and ineffective, got over their consternation, began to fire at the Indians who scattered, and individually beat a hasty escape in every direction.

CHAPTER SEVEN

SILVER CITY ON TIME

Butch did not slow the stage but continued the descent knowing that the miners' camp was large enough to fend for itself. In record time, they had reached the bottom and were moving easily along the trail to the Mimbres Valley before one last climb and the descent of the southern slopes of the Pinos Altos Range to Fort Bayard.

The stage stopped at Fort Bayard and Lieutenant Whiting stepped down. The Lieutenant was busy answering the excited questions of his fellow soldiers who gathered around the stage, looking at the scars of combat with the Warm Springs Apache. They tenderly removed the body of Trooper Jackson who had died during the last brush with Nana.

Butch was anxious to move on and cut short the good-byes being exchanged by Lilly and Lieutenant Whiting. The Lieutenant insisted that she meet him the following day at the Gateway Hotel in Silver City and she falsely promised to be there. At Butch's urging, the stage left Fort Bayard and headed toward Silver City with everyone forgetting that they still had the military mounts in harness.

An hour later, they turned into the main street of Silver City and headed for the south side of town where the North Star Stage terminal was located. In the middle of town, Banker Wilson called to the driver, "Stop the stage, I want out, stop the stage!"

He got out with his valise and gruffly said good-bye to all while grumbling, "Its criminal the horrible things I've had to endure." Lilly had bandaged the shoulder wound and it was no longer bleeding. He at least thanked Lilly and assured her that he would get immediate attention.

Two blocks later, the stage pulled into the station with Butch, Bartlett, the Marshal, and Lilly as its only passengers. It was getting dark and you could not see the ravages of the trip or guess at the condition of the people on board.

As they pulled into the stage yard, Marshal Doyle reached over and put his right hand atop the clasped hands of Lilly and said to her in a soft voice, "Little lady, I've watched the sacrifice you've made, and I want you to know that I'm a better man for having known you."

Lilly smiled in appreciation and looked at the Marshal and said, "Marshal, I thank you Sir, and I'm going to see if I can't start over."

Just then Troy Hatfield came out of the office looking at his watch and marveling as the stage pulled to a stop.

He yelled up to Butch, "By golly, Butch, you're a full half hour ahead of schedule. They ain't a kiddin' when they say this is the on-time stage line."

It was on time, but it was also the last time the North Star Stage would make a run, as the Mogollon Rim, along with the entire Southwest, became engulfed in the flames of the Warm Springs Rebellion.

CHAPTER EIGHT

BURNT WAGONS

Lilly was at the livery stable early the next morning seeking a ride westward. Liveryman Charlie Anson responded, "Only a fool would strike out in this country after what happened to the stage."

Lilly shot back at the liveryman, "I know all about the stage and I'm not afraid of anything that might lie ahead after what I've already been through."

She continued, "I've been to the stage station and they have canceled all trips westward. In fact," she said, "they've canceled everything in every direction."

Lilly was a beautiful sight in the dawn with her auburn hair shimmering in the sun with glints of fire.

Anson thought, here's a beautiful woman with a fine figure, and a straight, commanding carriage.

He wanted to be of help and suggested that she go down to the freight yard, "There might be a wagon train heading towards Mogollon."

The freight yard was a block down the street and as Lilly walked there she drew many an admiring gaze. A beautiful woman in a bustling boom town like Silver City was a rare object and a sight to be savored and enjoyed.

At the freight yards Lilly talked to Homer Hooten who met her inquiry with disbelief.

"You mean that you would risk your life traveling on one of these wagons to Mogollon after what's happened in this country?"

He shook his head and continued, "I'm having to pay one hundred dollars a man premium to these freighters to risk going through. How could it be worthwhile for you to take such a chance?"

Lilly told him that she had been on the stage under attack for the last five days and that she wanted to keep moving and the threat did not bother her. Homer marveled at her fortitude and courage and finally agreed to put her on a wagon to Mogollon for a twenty-five dollar fee.

Mogollon was a rip-snortin' mining town enjoying all of the excitement and confusion of a major mineral strike. The cowboys who were willing to risk their lives hauling the freight to Mogollon were doing it as much for the prospect of being in on the riches to be won in Mogollon as the one hundred dollars pay to see the wagons through.

There were six men on the three wagons that pulled out at 10:00 in the morning, first stopping by the hotel to gather Lilly's belongings. The small train pulled up the hill out of Silver City and headed west. The wagons were Studebaker freight wagons pulled by six mules each. They were heavily loaded with flour, lard, nails, bolts of cloth, hammers, saws, and all of the tools of the building trade, along with ammunition, guns, and many other items of hardware. This was a speculation load that Homer had gotten together knowing that everything he was shipping would command a premium price with the outbreak of Indian hostilities. The guns and ammunition he expected would sell at ten times their normal value.

The mules pulled hard on the first hill, the wagons heavily loaded. All of the men on the ground helped turn the wheels before reaching the summit. Lilly finally jumped off and walked to lighten the load of the wagon in which she rode. From the summit to Mangas Creek the road led mostly downhill and was an easy ride. The road was in good repair and it was a beautiful day. A sharp rain the day before had broken the drought, settling the dust, presenting a marvelous view to the north of the southern escarpment of the Mogollon Rim.

The Rim was a dark and brooding mass of land rising abruptly from the desert floor. It was gashed with deep, steep canyons cutting through the escarpment. Streaks of violet, magenta, and orange hinted at the heavy mineral content of the range.

As they traveled along, parallel to the Rim, Lilly told the drivers of her ordeal on the North Star Stage under attack by hostile

Apaches on the way to Silver City. The town that morning had been abuzz with stories of the stage's ordeal. In fact, one account had everyone on board dead. But, of course, Lilly disputed that. Besides being engrossed by the story of her adventures, they marveled at her good looks and friendly demeanor. These men, starved for the company of a woman, took full advantage of her presence.

They stopped under a large cottonwood at Mangas Creek and broke out the lunch vittles. As they ate, a surrey appeared, coming down the road from Silver City towards the parked wagons. When the surrey pulled up beside the wagons, Lilly gazed in surprise at the lone occupant of the buggy, Banker Wilson.

The drovers, when they learned that Wilson was heading for Mogollon, suggested that he travel with them.

He told them, "No, that will hold me back and I need to get there pronto." He finally looked over at Lilly and asked if she would care to accompany him.

She nodded her head immediately, and said, "Of course. You are so kind to ask. I would love to."

The drovers protested the prospect of Lilly traveling across the desolate country ahead with Apaches on the warpath, but they could not dissuade either Lilly or Banker Wilson from making the trip alone and unescorted.

Lilly laughingly responded, "Every Apache in the Gila is behind us. There can't be any more up front."

Lilly, with the help of one of the drovers, transferred her bags over to the second seat of the surrey, noticing that a blue carpetbag with a flower pattern was sitting on the seat, the same bag that Banker Wilson had guarded with more concern than he had for his own life throughout the ordeal on the stage coach. Lilly wondered again, as she had often during the stage trip, what might be in the bag that the banker protected so jealously.

With Lilly seated aboard the surrey, Wilson snapped his whip, and they moved out smartly. Wilson had rented the horse and buggy at the livery and had to put up a deposit of two hundred dollars because Charlie Anson did not want to risk either his horse equipment on such a hazardous journey. The horse, pulling the surrey, a solid, good-looking bay, could easily carry them to Mogollon if the Indians didn't intervene.

Off they went through a wild and pristine countryside. Rolling, grassy hills which would come to support some day a flourishing cattle industry. Off to the right rose the Mogollon Rim with its heavy mantle of dark timber. For a while the road traveled along Mangas Creek, named after the great Warm Springs Chief, "Mangas Coloradas."

In a few miles, the road left Mangas Creek and, after crossing low hills, dropped alongside the Gila River. Wilson had been warned at the livery stables that the crossing of the Gila was a dangerous one and not to attempt it with the river on the rise. When they reached the crossing, they found that the river was at a low stage and that the summer rains had not freshened it enough to create a hazard. Even at that, there was a time or two that the wheels began to sink in the shifting sand and Wilson had to pop his whip fiercely to encourage the horse to pull harder.

On the other side, the road continued through similar country until they reached the banks of the San Francisco River, finally camping for the night at a tributary of cold, rushing mountain water coming from the depths of the Mogollon Range. They made a cold camp and didn't start a fire because of possible Indian presence. They were up at first light resuming their journey. They did not try to catch any fish in the tributary but they could see the native Gila trout by the hundreds swimming in the clear waters.

Just after they had started out in the morning for Mogollon, they met a cavalry patrol consisting of an officer and eighteen men. It turned out they were the complement from Camp Vincent which had been abandoned at the start of hostilities. They had a lively conversation about recent events and the experiences Lilly and Banker Wilson had had on the North Star Stage. The lieutenant was shocked to learn that Trooper Jackson had been killed during the fight with the Apaches at Camp Sherman.

The visit was brief as the cavalry was in a hurry to reach Fort Bayard and receive new orders. The soldiers said good-bye to Lilly and Banker Wilson and hurried on to meet freight wagons that could not be far behind.

Soon after they left the cavalry, the road turned to the north and started up an incline into the Mogollon Range. It was a gentle pull at first but it became steeper and steeper, finally ending in a severe grade up a twisting canyon sometimes bottomed with an intermittent stream. At last, turning a corner, they entered the mining camp of Mogollon.

Mogollon was a community that stretched for almost a mile. However, it was one tent deep on each side of the precipitous canyon. There was barely room for a road to pass the fronts of the tents and the few wooden buildings that had been erected. The only hotel was a large tent where cots were available for five dollars a night. Blankets, hung on poles, were the only privacy. There were thirty cots in the tent and all were taken with the exception of three. It was obvious that there was no place for Lilly to stay as all of the occupants were men and there were no toilet facilities other than the brush outside.

While Lilly and Banker Wilson debated where they would sleep that night, a townsman, Ole Bratburg, a big tall Norwegian who had seen them talking to the hotel proprietor, spoke to Lilly and asked, "Can you wait tables?" When she said, "Certainly," he shot back, "Well, that's great, because I can give you a place to sleep with my wife and daughter in the back of our cafe if you'll go to work right now."

Lilly didn't ask the terms, conditions, or salary of her employment, she was so anxious to find a place where she could have some privacy. Her new employer hung Lilly's bags on the saddle pommel and, leading his horse, walked with Lilly to his restaurant where she was introduced to Engrid and Kirsten, his wife and daughter who were frantically preparing for the noon rush.

Lilly left Banker Wilson pondering his own fate after thanking him profusely for giving her a ride to Mogollon. Lilly put her belongings in the back room where she was to stay and promptly went to work helping the family meet the strenuous demands upon their enterprise. As soon as the noon rush was over, she was busy cleaning tables, sweeping the floors, and, then, doing the dishes.

The wife and daughter were right in there with her working as hard as she was. They were robust women used to work.

Lilly had no time to think of anything else but the work that she was engaged in when dinner rolled around and the crowd grew bigger. It resembled a stampede, with steaks selling for ten dollars apiece. Even at that price, there soon were none to serve. Ole had a hunter working full time bringing in venison, elk, and bear meat. Elk was the favorite and sold at the same price as beef. But when a man got hungry, he'd pay a big price for a venison steak and even the bear steaks sold for top dollar when other meat was not available.

While waiting on the evening diners, Lilly learned the terrible fate of the wagon train she had been on. The cavalry patrol had found them all massacred on the banks of the Gila River and had returned to Mogollon with the damaged wagons and the bodies of the victims. They had been attacked by a large band of Warm Springs under Mangas, the younger son of the famous chief. The Indians had taken the guns and ammunition and set the wagons on fire. The cavalry patrol interrupted the carnage and prevented the ransacking of the rest of the cargo.

Lilly was disheartened. She had liked the drovers and felt that she had lost her own family. She thanked God she had not shared their fate, and yet she felt guilty for having accepted Banker Wilson's invitation.

The Indians had attacked the wagons as they started to cross the Gila River. Little Mangas had twenty braves with him. They had watched from ambush as Banker Wilson and Lilly crossed the river. They were only interested in the wagons and the potential cargo they contained, particularly guns and ammunition.

The Indians had hidden in a growth of willows fifty yards upstream from the cut in the bank where the wagons were to cross and when the lead wagon had been committed to the crossing, fell upon the drovers. Three of the drovers died with the first fusillade of shots and arrows and the other three fought valiantly before being overwhelmed in a hand-to-hand encounter.

The Indians quickly opened the rifle boxes, distributed them.

Each one took all the ammunition he could carry and retreated, leaving the field to the cavalry. The initial ease in which the Warm Springs acquired not only horses but guns and ammunition, inspired them to believe that they could prevail against the whites.

CHAPTER NINE  THE WHISKEY BUSINESS

The next ten days were the hardest Lilly had ever worked in her life. As news of the Warm Springs uprising spread, miners who were scattered far and wide throughout the Gila heard of the danger and sought shelter in the mining and ranching communities. In the western Gila below the Mogollon Rim, the closest towns were Reserve and Mogollon. Mogollon being a mining camp, they naturally preferred this location and the small boom town was filled beyond its limits.

The restaurant did a rush business and, at any time of the day or night, there might be a line outside the tent stretching down the street. It wasn't a question of whether you wanted to eat there, there was just no other place to eat unless you had your own food, and that was rare.

The proprietor of the restaurant was from Tooten, Norway. Ole had been raised on the Bratburg Farm. His family name had been Olson and his wife's family name had also been Olson. After immigrating to the United States they settled in Fairview, Minnesota. They found that there were twenty-seven Ole Olsons in the small community. In order to be distinguishable from such a large family, they changed their name to Bratburg, the same as the family farm.

While the ladies kept the restaurant going, Ole bought a wagon and a team of horses and headed for Silver City to get provisions to keep their business going. The ladies were alarmed at the idea and did everything they could to talk him out of it but to no avail. He recruited four miners to go with him who were giving up the ghost of ever making a big strike and off they went to Silver City. In ten days, Ole was safely back loaded down with everything it took to operate a restaurant except for meat, which his hunter was providing.

Lilly didn't know it at the time, but Mr. Bratburg had bought his wagon and team from Banker Wilson. When Lilly and Banker Wilson had parted company and Lilly had gone to work for Mr. Bratburg, Banker Wilson entered into negotiations with the owner of the livery stable where they had first stopped when arriving at Mogollon. The livery stable also served as the headquarters for the stage traveling west to Arizona. With the Indian uprising on and the stage shut down, things looked pretty bleak for the livery business so Banker Wilson was able to strike a good bargain and bought the whole shebang, buildings, horses, corrals, two coaches, the office, living quarters, and, what he wanted most, a large safe.

The owner of the livery stable, Barth Coldwell, wanted cash in gold coin. Banker Wilson, excusing himself, asked if he could go out to the outhouse for a minute and Coldwell thought it was strange that he carried his blue carpetbag with him. In a minute, he returned and paid Coldwell off two thousand five hundred dollars in twenty-dollar gold pieces. Coldwell suspiciously bit into a coin to be sure he had been fairly paid. Satisfied, he began to wonder how he was going to get the gold back to Silver City with the Indian war that was going on. Banker Wilson and Coldwell penned the deed and bill of sale and, with everything signed, sealed, and delivered, they negotiated rent for a week for Coldwell to stay on the premises. As a result, Banker Wilson had a warm bed his first night in Mogollon, sleeping in a wood framed building, one of four in the town.

Two days later, when the cavalry brought the wagons in that had belonged to the drovers killed at the Gila Crossing, Banker Wilson signed a receipt for the wagons and all the goods that were left. This satisfied the army lieutenant who wanted to clear the problem of taking care of the personal property from his own hands. Wilson set up an account and scrupulously kept track of everything that came in from the sale of the commodities and fully intended to pay the rightful owner when he became identified.

Wilson had heard that there was a beautiful red headed woman serving the tables at the Bratburg Cafe at the north end of town and, a week after his arrival, decided to have dinner there.

Lilly was very surprised to see her buggy mate and enthusiastically embraced him. After he told her that he was the owner of the livery stable and the stage line and that he had bought the goods from the wagons, she wondered what in the world is he doing in Mogollon? She couldn't understand why he had left Magdalena, he never mentioned Magdalena or his wife, or the bank. Being true to the code of the West, she never asked any questions.

Three days later, Ole Bratburg was back in town with his wagon loaded and the restaurant continued its unbelievable business. Within a month, Ole had made more money than he ever thought there was in the whole world and the Bratburgs had ratholed under the dirt floor of the sleeping tent almost three thousand five hundred dollars. A small fortune.

News had spread throughout the camp that a group of twenty prospectors had purchased wagons from Wilson and were going to travel in strength to Arizona where there were reported strikes of silver and gold and Indians were said to be still docile. Engrid begged her husband, "Ole lets take this money and move on. We have enough now to be successful anywhere," adding, "besides, were going to be scalped if we stay here."

Ole was inclined to grant his wife's wish. He hated to leave such a thriving business unless he could sell at a decent price.

Lilly overheard him propositioning some of the customers to buy him out and the next day during her morning break she went down the street to the livery stable to see Wilson. When she told Wilson, "The Bratburg's are going to move on if they can get a thousand dollars for the restaurant, can you lend me eight hundred fifty dollars to go with the one hundred and fifty I've saved?" Wilson accommodated, "I couldn't make a better investment and I sure as hell owe you a favor."

Two days later, the Bratburg's pulled out with the miners heading west and Lilly became the sole owner of a thriving mining camp business. Lilly's business continued to boom. Her only trouble was finding help and the luck of the hunter in bringing in game. She hired a second hunter and, with help from Wilson, had three wagonloadss of provisions freighted in from Silver City, fortunately, without attack from the Indians.

Some of the miners were leaving town and heading back for the diggings, thinking that the Indian scare was all over. But for every man who left, two newcomers came to town having heard of the rich strikes being made in the area.

One day, Wilson came into the cafe and asked to see Lilly privately for a moment. They stepped into the back quarters and Wilson told Lilly, "You can do better if you opened a saloon next door."

There were three saloons in town, but they were only tents with wooden boards for a bar and terrible reputations for the rot gut whiskey they served.

Wilson continued, "On those wagons I bought were all kinds of carpenter tools, and there's a few carpenters in town." Lilly nodded her head and Wilson proposed, "I'll buy the land next door and build a wooden saloon that connects to your restaurant." He proposed that they be half partners in the saloon and that he put up the money and that she provide the know-how. Lilly responded, "It's a deal!"

The clapboard construction went up in less than a month with a grand celebration in Mogollon in honor of the first real indoor saloon with swinging doors. The roaring town popped its cork that night, and there wasn't a sober person to be seen except for six Chinese who had come to town from El Paso to open up a laundry.

Opening night saw the first good whiskey served in Mogollon. Lilly and Wilson had spirits shipped by rail from El Paso to Deming and then by wagon from Deming to Silver City and on to Mogollon. They were charging a twenty-dollar gold piece for a bottle of champagne and, as the evening wore on, miners were spending their twenty-dollar gold pieces as if they were dimes, toasting everything they could think of with champagne. Even Lilly got a little tipsy, but not so that she didn't keep her eye on everything that was going on.

Between her and Wilson, they didn't miss much. There might have been a bartender or two make an extra dollar that night, but not enough to dim the future of what was going to be better than any gold mine.

Lilly told Wilson, "The secret of any bar business is to have some girls around the place to encourage the patrons to spend their money." Wilson agreed and hired a guard of six men for a trip to El Paso where Lilly recruited bar maids. She had no trouble finding plenty of girls eager to go to Mogollon when she offered wages three times what they were paying in El Paso. She was honest with them and told them there was going to be danger but they were anxious to try their fortune in the booming town of Mogollon.

Two weeks after the girls had arrived, Lilly found two of them propositioning the customers to go outside and enjoy their favors for a gold eagle. Lilly angrily told Wilson what had happened. Wilson realized that here was an opportunity for great wealth. He propositioned Lilly, "Let's expand the business to include a sporting house separate and apart from the restaurant and bar."

At first Lilly was reluctant, but reasoned to herself, there's a fortune to be made and if I don't make it, someone else will. She agreed and she and Banker Wilson sealed their agreement with a hearty shake.

Banker Wilson's carpenters put up a large building on a ridge directly above the middle of town. While the building was going up, Lilly made the trip back to El Paso with one of the girls she had caught trying to promote her own business and soon had ten girls from Utah Street, the red light district in El Paso, ready to come back to Mogollon. Utah Street had a dozen bordellos doing a dandy business at the time.

Lilly had a run-in with one of the madams on Utah Street who caught her proselytizing her girls. The madam, without warning, attacked Lilly, pulling her hair and scratching her face. Lilly backed off and yelled out, "No you don't," and cocked her right hand and delivered an uppercut which sent Madam Cline flying backward, out cold, before she hit the deck. Lilly picked up the nickname of "Champ" as a result of this encounter and closed off her recruiting drive and returned to Mogollon with her prizes.

The toughest of the girls who had gone to work for Lilly was Lupe Rivera who had the respect of all and could handle any drunken man who was looking for trouble. Lilly put Lupe in charge and confined her management talents to checking the money and keeping the accounts as business boomed as never before. As the only sporting house in the Gila, news of its presence spread far and wide.

Everything was going fine. There had been almost two months with no news of Indian depredations and business was booming in all three of Lilly's ventures when, suddenly, the Apache threat bore down on Mogollon.

CHAPTER TEN

A DEAD MINER

Apache raiding became so intense along the road from Silver City to Mogollon that it required a major force of men to provide any security. The town, however, continued to grow as strikes were made and more miners poured in. The business in the saloon was phenomenal. There was a problem, however, with the drunks wanting to shoot off their guns and the fights that come with any bar operation. Lilly was happy when she heard that the federal government was sending a Marshal into town to cool things off.

The day the Marshal arrived, Lilly hurried down to the livery station where he was going to make his headquarters and was delighted to find that it was none other than her old friend Joe Doyle.

When Lilly walked into the office of the livery stable, Joe looked up and couldn't believe his eyes. Sure enough, there was Lilly, just as big as life. He jumped up and ran across the room and grabbed her by both shoulders and actually picked her up off the floor saying, "By golly, I can't believe it! It's wonderful to see you."

Lilly blushed, stammered for a moment, and finally replied, "Joe, you're a godsend, and a sight for sore eyes. How have you been?"

Joe replied, "I've been helping the Marshal in Silver City. I heard you were in Mogollon."

Banker Wilson joined Joe and Lilly as they excitedly shared their lives since the last ride on the North Star Stage. The Marshal had come into town by horseback and had brought warrants with him to build a jail and office. He quickly cut a deal with Banker Wilson and, before the first nail had been driven in a plank for the new facility, he had an occasion to make his presence known in the community. He had arrived in town on a Thursday and Saturday night Lilly sent one of her bartenders out the back door with instructions, "Find the Marshal and get him here quick."

The place had been brim full and a major poker game had

gotten under way. There were seven contestants. Six of them miners and one, a cowboy, from a ranch over by Alma. The cowboy had used the name of Chris when he joined the game and he had three companions with him. During the course of the evening, he made it known that he was the foreman of a ranch and had been there about a year. One of his friends watched the poker game propped back on a chair leaning on the wall while the other two cowboys were at the bar drinking.

If the miners had known they were playing poker with an accomplished gunman, trouble would never have developed. But as the night wore on, the drinks dulled good sense and resentment began to rise over the winnings that Chris amassed.

One of the miners in particular became obnoxious and had called for two new decks and said directly to Chris, "It just doesn't figure to be honest for a guy to have the run of luck you're havin'."

Chris kept his cool, smiled, and said, "Well, its about time I had a little luck, because I'm normally the doormat in these games."

It was then that Lilly had sent for the Marshal. As the Marshal came in the back door, the trouble she had worried about erupted.

Chris had just won a big pot when the miner, Mike Milligan, his face growing blood red, said, "God damn it, you're a cheat!" With that exclamation, he stood up, reaching for his gun. Marshal Doyle from thirty feet away interrupted the play and, drawing, put a slug through the left eye of Milligan, killing him instantly. As Milligan slumped over the table, dead, the Marshal stood with his gun steady waiting to see if anyone else wanted instant justice.

Chris yelled, "Marshal, don't shoot. I need to holster my gun."

With that, Chris pushed his chair back and everyone could see that during the episode, he had a forty-four under the table trained squarely on Milligan.

Chris holstered his weapon and turned to the Marshal and said, "Can I buy you a drink Law Man."

As the two men walked to the bar, Lilly directed two of the bartenders, "Take him into the back room while I send word to the town undertaker to get over here."

When the two men reached the bar, they each ordered a shot of whiskey and the Marshal looked at Chris and said, "It looks like you didn't even need me."

Chris replied, "Maybe not Marshal, but I'm sure glad you came. If I had stretched him out, his friends would have been demanding my hide."

Doyle replied, "Yeah, that's right. But I sure do admire your cool. I wouldn't mind having you around to back my play."

With that compliment, Chris broke out in a great big smile, and said, "Well, I'm just a plain ol' cowboy, and I don't 'magine I'll ever see you again, but I sure owe you a big one. Let me buy you another drink. I need to get back to the ranch. The boss let us come to town tonight, but he's awful worried about Indians and we told him we'd be back before midnight." The two downed another round with the quick jerk and gulp of a Westerner and, turning toward each other, shook hands. Joe Doyle never knew it but there was three thousand dollars in reward money in his hand that night.

Word quickly spread through the camp that the new Marshal was for real. And there was also considerable speculation that it would be foolish to call "Cowboy Chris" a cheat.

Throughout the excitement, one of Chris' friends had never changed his position with his chair leaning against the wall. What no one in the place had seen, except Lilly, was that when Milligan stood up to make his play, the friend had already cleared leather and was ready to blow a hole in the back of Milligan's head when the Marshal's shot beat him to the punch. Milligan was a loud-mouthed bully and when he finally drew his death card it was in spades, with three guns ready to blast him to hell.

Chris and his companions left Mogollon that night for a four hour ride back to the ranch and into utter oblivion as far as Mogollon was concerned. They never made another trip to the mining camp or any other New Mexico town before moseying on.

It was several weeks before Marshal Doyle again had to resort to his pistol to keep the peace. Not that he wasn't frequently called upon to calm down a boisterous drunk or step between two would- be combatants. The Apache depredations became more severe.

The Army rushed more troops into the area while the Apaches countered by mobilizing every man, woman, and child and, in desperation, invented guerilla warfare.

CHAPTER ELEVEN

WHITING COMES TO TOWN

As part of the military build up, a troop of cavalry was stationed at Mogollon. A week before their arrival, a wagon train coming in from Silver City had brought the news that the Army was sending troops to Mogollon to protect the town from Indian raids. And "none too soon" was the consensus of the mining community as, the week before. eight miners had been wiped out at a placer mine just six miles north of Mogollon. Everyone believed that dreaded Geronimo, himself, had led the attack.

Many of the townspeople were on hand to welcome the military contingent to town but Lilly was not among them, being busy taking care of her booming business.

The afternoon the troops arrived, Lilly drove up the hill to see how things were going at her bordello locally known as "Fanny Hill." She had a long visit with Lupe and offered to make her a partner with a one-fifth interest in the business.

Wilson and Lilly had decided this was the best way to keep the services of Lupe who had proved to be indispensable at running the house. Lupe had taken up the offer providing they could open a second establishment. They were so busy at the first that they had a waiting line and Lupe was having trouble with the girls. The Anglo girls didn't get along with the Mexican girls and vice versa. She was constantly having to calm things down and, at least once a week, break up a rip-roaring fight between the prostitutes who were extremely jealous of each other because of the commission system that Lupe had them working on. A good girl with a little get-up-and-go and sales ability had a chance to make a small fortune the way money was flowing in Mogollon. With the Apache problems, there were no other women in town so there was not much choice for a male who wanted female company but to climb up to "Fanny Hill".

Lupe wanted to separate the warring factions and name the new place "Spanish Town". A bargain was struck. Driving her buggy back to Mogollon Lilly passed by the encampment where the troops were preparing to bivouac and couldn't believe her eyes when she saw Lieutenant Whiting supervising the activities.

She parked the buggy and called, "Lieutenant, Lieutenant! Come here, it's Lilly."

Whiting recognized the voice as Lilly's. He had thought of nothing but her since the ordeal on the North Star Stage. He had asked everywhere the next day in Silver City about her but all he could find out was that she had checked out of the hotel in the morning. At the railroad depot he had been told that a girl resembling Lilly had taken the train to Deming and he assumed she was gone from his life forever. He was very disappointed as no girl had ever affected him so.

He ran to where Lilly was and, as she jumped from the buggy, he embraced her with great relish. She responded eagerly. While their lips didn't touch, the body contact had both of their hearts racing. Lilly didn't tell Whiting about her business on the hill but did tell him about her restaurant and bar and that she was Wilson's partner. She also told him that Doyle was in town and had done a great job taming the community.

Whiting finally remembered that he had soldiers to take care of and gave directions to Sergeant Baskind on how to set up the camp. He apologized to Lilly for being busy.

She responded, "I understand but you must visit me tonight at my place the 'North Star'."

Whiting replied, "I'll be there."

She smiled and said, "If you don't come down there, Lieutenant, I'm gonna come out here and make you my prisoner."

He laughed and said, "Don't worry, I'm going to be there with bells on."

True to his word, he saddled up and was tying his horse to the rail in front of the saloon when his watch showed 7:30. He went inside and marveled at the business that was going on. Several other saloons had tried to start up, but none of them could compete with Lilly's. There were a half-dozen attractive young women, dressed in flounced skirts, waiting on tables, and taking turns at entertaining the crowd. There were four bartenders on duty and kerosene chandeliers hanging everywhere.

When he walked in he could see Lilly standing at the end of the bar in a beautiful blue dress. It was the only one in the house that came below the knees. Her auburn hair was down and flowing to her waist. She was the most beautiful woman Whiting had ever seen.

When Lilly saw Whiting coming across the room, her heart raced and she clenched her fists saying softly to herself, "You gotta keep control. Don't be a fool. You just gotta keep control."

Lilly had been chaste for six months. Ever since Banker Wilson had helped her start up her own business she had been working too hard to even think of having a fling. She had her share of romance anyway when she was working in bars and had found out the hard way that liquor aroused her passion and her sympathy made her a sitting duck for a sad story from a cowboy. When she and Wilson had opened the bar, she knew that she could never be a success by drinking up the profits.

Whiting came over and grabbed both of her arms in greeting, saying, "Gosh you're beautiful, I just can't get over your being here."

Lilly's face flushed at the compliment and she ordered a bottle of Champagne to a corner table reserved for her. Alfonse, the bartender, brought out two chairs from behind the bar and Lilly and the Lieutenant sat down.

Lilly told him all about her business success and how wonderful Joe Doyle had been on many occasions. The two relived their dangerous days together on the North Star Stage regretting the deaths of Zacharias Smith and Troopers Jackson and Price. And, of course, they wondered about Billy Joe. Had he made good on his escape? He had not been heard of nor seen by any of his stagecoach companions, not knowing the wolves had scattered his bones.

In no time they had downed the bottle of Champagne, neither of them being aware of their rapid consumption. Alfonse was watching Lilly and the Lieutenant and he could tell that Lilly was smitten by the young man. He had not seen her display any emotion before towards anyone. He liked her very much and was anxious to please her so the minute the champagne bottle was empty he had another bottle cold and ready to take its place.

Lilly always closed the bar at 1:00 in the morning. Not that there was any law in the New Mexico territory that required closing but she felt it was just common sense to shut down because people were by then well along the road to having too much to drink and many had already left. This particular night, when 1:00 a.m. came, the bartender, as usual, shut the bar down and suggested to the stragglers that they better get home if they wanted to enjoy their day off tomorrow.

When the last customer was gone, Alfonse finished turning out all the lights with the exception of the lamp on the table where Lilly and Whiting were still, with great animation, talking to each other. Lilly thanked him and threw the latch behind him as he went out the front door.

She returned to Whiting and, lifting her glass, drank the last of the champagne. Whiting did likewise and, in the soft light of the lantern, told her, "I just don't want to leave."

Lilly turned her head and in a low soft voice said, "I don't want you to."

She turned back to face him as he placed his lips on hers embracing her with passion. She responded with all of the emotion she possessed, forcing her hips forward. The alcohol had done its job and she was a tiger on the prowl.

When finally they broke off the embrace, blowing out the lamp Lilly took Whiting by the hand and led him up to her quarters. When they were in her room, she did not strike a new light but instead turned to him and began to unbutton his jacket. The next day he would wonder about her confidence and composure but that night nothing crossed his mind but the prospect of possessing Lilly.

When she had unbuttoned his jacket, he quickly took it off and fumbled with the buttons on his shirt before she had a chance. Lilly grasped his hands in hers and, instead, led them to her own blouse. Clumsily, he tried to undo the buttons. Lilly sensed his lack of experience and undid them herself and next slipped from her dress. Whiting, by then, had taken his own shirt off and stood trembling in eagerness. Lilly unbuckled his belt, slipped her hands inside his trousers and, reaching down, massaged firmly. Whiting couldn't wait. He was afraid that if something didn't happen immediately, it might be too late.

He pulled her hands up and quickly took off his boots and trousers. Lilly had by then undressed and the two stood pressed together for a moment embracing before Lilly turned and led him through the dark of the room to the bed. There was no foreplay. Whiting claimed his prize and penetrated Lilly with such frenzy that she cried out, momentarily shocked, but, like her partner, totally abandoned to the joy of union. Their excitement raced to extremes that neither had ever known before and, at culmination, Whiting's entire psyche was pulsating with the rhythm of their embrace.

Maddened, the rhythm hurried, the rhythm, the rhythm, pulsing, celebrating their unbridled passion.

Throughout the night they embraced, spoke words of love and devotion. They were both gentle and forceful, each with the other, giving erotic license to their desire.

CHAPTER TWELVE  A SICK LIEUTENANT

The next morning when Lilly awakened, the champagne was pounding in her head. Sunlight was streaming in the window, falling on the bed and there she was, still naked, lying beside Whiting. She belatedly realized she had not taken any precaution and Whiting had shown no forbearance. She thought, *If I'm not pregnant after last night, I will never be.* As she put on her chemise and began to dress, she didn't care. What had happened to her that night was worth any sacrifice, any price.

She wondered, *Is it possible to marry the Lieutenant?* After all, she had closed the gap on his respectability by amassing a small fortune in her business endeavors and Whiting knew nothing about her past. *Why shouldn't I claim all the happiness I can in life?* Lilly finished dressing without waking the Lieutenant and slipped from the room and, going downstairs, had the cook prepare a breakfast tray. By the time she got back, Whiting had awakened and was half dressed when she came in the room with hot coffee and scrambled eggs and bacon.

Whiting looked at Lilly and blurted out, "This kind of service sure beats the Army." They ate breakfast together with scarcely a word passing but, with their eyes locked on each other, there was no need for words to tell of the appreciation they both felt for the night before.

When breakfast was over, Whiting stood up and went over to where Lilly was sitting, and bent down and kissed her gently full on the mouth. She parted her lips and let their tongues touch.

The Lieutenant quickly drew back and looked at Lilly and said, "I have a troop waiting for me, I must leave."

She looked back and nodded her head and said, "I understand. Be back tonight."

He nodded in assurance and left the room.

Whiting let himself out the front door of the saloon and was dismayed to find that his horse was not there. He, of course, should never have left the horse tied to a post all night like that.

The horse had either pulled itself loose or someone had untied it. The Lieutenant quickly began the walk to where his troop was bivouacked. When he got there, he found that Sergeant Baskind had been the good soldier he always was and had breakfasted the men and had them ready to mount. Fortunately, a commissary wagon had accompanied them and they had a few extra saddles and there were spare mounts. Baskind quickly outfitted the Lieutenant and the patrol out for Summit Creek Divide.

The first ten miles were a very steep climb with constant switch-backs following an old Indian trail which led from the top of the Mogollon Rim down the western escarpment to the plains below. The troop stopped every half hour and walked their mounts for ten minutes to give them relief and to give the pack train a chance to catch up. The mules were small and slower than the horses.

The Lieutenant tried to think about his mission and the need to find out where the Apaches were and their strength but all thought of duty was blotted out by the memory of what had happened the night before. As he relived it in his mind, there was always the nagging question, why had she been so confident? How did she know as much as she knew? She was far more experienced than himself. In the back of his mind, his male pride asked the nagging question, *Why had she become the aggressor?*

How could she be so accomplished? There was only one answer. She had known many men.

When this thought would cross his mind, the sheer ecstacy of the night of love would overcome his baser instincts and he would think, No! It was just because he was in love and she was in love and it was the right moment.

All day long the battle raged within him. When the horses and men grew tired so did the resolve of Whiting and he began to think that he had been duped and made a fool of. If that was true and she told everyone around town what a fool he was, surely the men would learn and then what would happen to his role as leader, what would happen to the men in his charge if they despised him. There was, of course, no basis for any of these fears but they mounted and magnified in his mind until, by the time they reached the Divide, he was thoroughly despondent.

At the Divide, they broke into two groups moving to the northeast and northwest, covering the main east-west trails across the Gila. There was no recent sign of Indian activity anywhere and, after spending the night, they returned to Mogollon late the next afternoon. Whiting wanted to go to the saloon and see Lilly but he knew if he did he would be unable to resist her invitation. And now, having thoroughly convinced himself that he was a fool and being used and that the whole world would soon know of his amateurish assignation, he was determined to resist. He left Lilly alone to wonder what had happened to her soldier boy.

Lilly sent her trusted friend and employee, Alfonse, to see if the troop had returned and it was 10:00 when he came back and said, yes, that they were camped at the other edge of town. The next morning, Lilly got in her buggy and drove to the camp. Sergeant Baskind saw the buggy turn in off the road and went to greet her. Sergeant Baskind had been with Whiting three years and had shared the stage adventures with Lilly. He was very happy to have a chance to visit her and accepted her welcoming hug with appreciation.

When she asked about the Lieutenant, Baskind lied and replied, "The Lieutenant is ill and wants no visitors." This was the story the Lieutenant had concocted anticipating that Lilly would come to the camp looking for him. Baskind was none too happy with his detail of deceit but he was a good soldier and for whatever reason the Lieutenant was resorting to falsehoods, he did his duty. Lilly knew from Baskind's nervous demeanor that there was something wrong and she persisted that she be allowed to see the Lieutenant and Baskind insisted no, that he had his orders.

Lilly felt that the one chance she had in life for true happiness was about to slip away and, in reaction, brushed past Baskind and ran to the Lieutenant's tent bursting in on him, found him sitting on his cot fully clothed and, of course, not in the least bit ill.

He jumped to his feet and stammered, "Lilly, what are you doing here?"

Lilly replied, "I was told you were ill." Her voice faltered, and then she said, "I think it is me who is ill and I have been so for a long time." She spun, her tresses flying, and left the tent and raced to her buggy.

Whiting waited for a second and then ran after her yelling, "Lilly, wait. Lilly, we need to talk."

By then Lilly was laying her whip on the back of the horse who bolted forward leaving Whiting behind, stammering and trying to collect his wits. Then he realized that the whole troop was watching him. They had seen everything. He had worried about playing the fool and by himself, without help from anyone, had taken on the role. He returned to his tent and stayed there the rest of the day. Baskind knew what was wrong and tried reasoning with him by saying, "Go to town. Find Lilly and tell her you love her." Whiting, however, had to much macho to bend his knee.

Whiting stayed in Mogollon for thirty more days and, when the patrol was over having made no contact with Apache, he left town without once trying to see Lilly.

Lilly kept hoping he would come through the door of the saloon, that he would knock on the back door of her quarters, that he would send her a message, or that something would happen. Anything! She instinctively knew he was bothered by her obvious experience and his pride had obliterated his judgment.

Had there been any hope of Whiting coming to his senses it was destroyed the day before he departed for Silver City when he went in to say good-bye to Wilson.

Wilson began to brag about all the money he was making and told him that he and Lilly had the three best businesses in town, including the whore houses on top of the hill. Whiting was appalled to learn of Lilly's ventures on the hill and the rigidity of the West Point training bucked up his resolve to cast her aside.

Whiting had been gone two months when Lilly knew for sure that her worst suspicions had been realized. She had missed two periods and hastily visited the town doctor. He confirmed that she was probably pregnant and gave her instructions on diet and activities. She hardly heard the doctor as he told her what she should and shouldn't do. She had already done what she shouldn't do. And she knew well that what she would have to do now was going to be painful and embarrassing.

CHAPTER THIRTEEN  A WEDDING

Six weeks later, Marshal Joe Doyle came in the saloon without his badge on. This meant he was there as a customer to relax and enjoy an evening playing cards and talking to Lilly and his many friends. Lilly was happy to see her friend and confidant and asked some miners at her corner table to move to the front so she could sit there with Joe. She treated to a bottle of champagne and, when the bottle was near gone, she confessed to Joe that she was in a real predicament, confessing, "I believe I'm pregnant."

She told him what had happened and said, "I'm going to go to Wilson and sell out and try my hand further to the west." Doyle was shocked at what Lilly told him. He had been in love with her from first sight and had no problem with her background. He would have been her eager suitor if he were younger. He urged her to think it over.

"Things aren't that bad. The Lieutenant will come back." He added, "I'll see to that tomorrow, bright and early. The Lieutenant will be back here hanging by his ears with a shotgun in his back if need be."

He continued, "Don't worry, we'll get that soldier boy back here doing his duty." Doyle growled, remembering Banker Wilson's words on the Stage, the Army is full of damn fools. *Well,* he thought, *Whiting is sure one of them.*

Lilly would have none of this. She protested, "I'll kill myself before I let you do such a stupid thing. The only answer is to get out of town as quickly as possible."

Lilly made the Marshal promise he wouldn't do anything and he agreed that he would obey her wish, and then he said, "And besides, you don't have to leave town. All you have to do is get married."

Lilly quickly responded, "In this condition, I couldn't ask anyone to marry me."

Doyle reached over and put a hand on each shoulder and shook her gently and said, "Look at me. I'd be glad to see you through this. Just say the word and we'll have the dangest wedding party this town has ever seen. And no one will ever know that I'm really not your husband."

Lilly shook her head sadly, and said, "No, I'll not let you be a damned fool for my sake." She continued, "Joe, you're the best friend I have and that friendship means too much to me to make such a mistake."

Joe protested, "No, this is what I want to do, and I'm gonna do it. Tomorrow I'm gonna let this whole town know that we're getting married."

They parted that night with Lilly firmly convinced that she had changed his mind and that he had gotten the notion out of his head.

But when they parted, Joe Doyle had an entirely different idea in his head. He was a man of action. A decision maker, and he knew that Lilly would have a tough time wherever she went bearing the ordeal of having a child and not being married. Convention bore down heavily and he knew that Lilly needed help and needed it fast.

The next morning he went through Mogollon, first down one side of the street and then back the other telling every person he met that he and Lilly were to be married next week and that the whole town was invited to the biggest celebration ever had in the Territory of New Mexico.

Doyle went to the saloon to make wedding plans and was dismayed to find that Lilly, acting on the Marshal's advise to get married, had left during the night with Alfonse, the bartender. No one knew where they had gone. The mystery was solved a week later when Lilly and Alfonse returned from Silver City as husband and wife. The Marshal felt betrayed, in no way mollified by the knowledge that Lilly thought she had acted in his best interest.

The Marshal concluded, *I'll never understand women, they have a different drumbeat than men.*

News of the wedding spread throughout the countryside and made the paper at Silver City where Lieutenant Whiting read the account and spent the day in bad humor. He had no inkling that this was a marriage of convenience to cover up the birth of his own child.

It was a marriage of convenience and Lilly continued the chastity she had assumed since coming to Mogollon except for the one evening with Whiting. Alfonse was true to his word. He was Lilly's husband as far as the community was concerned but never once suggested or made any demand upon her that she, in fact, be a wife. There were times when Lilly wanted to slip into his bed and thank him for being such a good man but she could never bring herself to it, believing that she would be demeaning him in the process.

CHAPTER FOURTEEN

MINER AMBUSH

The whites drove the Warm Springs from their Gila homeland forcing them to take refuge deep into the most desolate regions of the Gila where inaccessibility was keeping the whites out. From here they made raids for guns, horses, and ammunition.

Lilly continued to expand her enterprises and, with Banker Wilson, went into an extensive building program. The restaurant was now a solid building with a brick front and wooden walls, a main dining room and three private dining rooms, and a large kitchen with living quarters in back. The restaurant connected to the saloon which had been completely rebuilt and expanded until it was now one of the largest and most opulent in the Southwest. The two brothels were also flourishing. Lupe was managing them so well that Lilly hardly had to look at the books. Of course, Banker Wilson had such a sharp eye at figures that she really needn't bother.

Wilson had opened a bank in Mogollon and with his lucrative stage business and interest in Lilly's ventures, had become one of the wealthiest men in the Southwest. As prosperity continued, Lilly became heavy with child and, at the insistence of Wilson and Joe Doyle, in her eighth month moved to Silver City to be near a hospital and medical assistance.

On the trip to Silver City, Lilly didn't concern herself about the possibility of Apache attack as it had been almost six months since the last depredation in the Mogollon vicinity. It was, therefore, quite a surprise that when they reached the Gila River, the very spot where her friends, the wagon train members, had been killed by Mangas, she encountered a party of miners camped on the river bank where her friends had been ambushed and slain.

It was almost nightfall and the miners had just made camp after coming down the Gila River. It was a group of twenty-five who had made a sally into the heart of the Gila on a cooperative venture. They had banded together in such a large number to be safe from Indian attack and had agreed in advance by written contract to share the rewards of their venture. Unfortunately, the only thing they had to share was a month of bitter cold and frustration in the Gila.

The lower reaches of the Gila were devoid of any economic mineral potential and this was the last major expedition to go into the area in search of fame and fortune. They had, however, quite by accident delivered a bitter blow to the hopes of the Warm Springs in their effort to protect their homelands.

Two of the miners had gone up Iron Creek from the main camp looking for float in the stream bed when they suddenly came across a carcass of a deer which had recently been butchered. They recognized the signs of Indian activity as only the haunches had been removed. The Indians were well versed in survival in the Gila and knew that the best technique for provisioning their camp after a kill was to carry off the portions that had the most efficient combination of meat and weight, then return for more meat if they needed it.

The two miners immediately left the stream bottom and sought safety on the ridge to their right. They continued upstream just long enough to spot the Indian camp and determine that there were about fifteen braves and the same number of women and children preparing their evening meal. The two miners slipped back to their own camp and announced to their friends that there was a good size party of Apache five miles up Iron Creek.

A council of war was held and it was decided to attack the Indians at dawn. The miners divided into two forces. One proceeded directly up the canyon while the other stayed on the ridge to the right. The Apaches had no escape route on the left ridge as the canyon side was a sheer vertical wall.

The miners coming up the canyon bottom had given the party on the ridge a half an hour start. It had been agreed that the miners on the ridge would station themselves out at intervals and be in position to pick off the Indians attempting to escape when the main group in the canyon bottom made their attack. Jeff Smith, one of the miners who had found the Indian camp, was with the group in the valley while his friend, Bob Miller, was with the group on the ridge line.

The Indians were totally surprised. This was a place where they had never been harassed and, when the sun began to rise, they carelessly went about their early morning routines. When the sun burst over the canyon rim, the miners in the canyon attacked, pushing upstream with all of their weapons at rapid fire. The surprise was complete and there was no way that organized resistance could be put into effect. It was every man, woman, and child for himself. And the Indians scattered up the canyon. Some climbing the ridge. Others going along the stream itself. A few even tried to climb the cliffs to the left.

Those who tried to climb the cliffs were quickly picked off by the miners on the heights to the right. Those who had broken to the slope to the right of the camp soon realized they were heading right towards the ambushing whites and had to retrace their steps. They were annihilated. The only successful escapes were those Indians who went directly upstream and they, four in number, made it unscathed.

The miners overran the main camp and dispatched the wounded Indians without mercy. One of the miners in the group in the canyon was a big Irishman named Patrick O'Rourke. O'Rourke was as good an Indian hater as any man but he was also a pushover for anyone in trouble or at a disadvantage. When he burst into one of the makeshift wickiups and found a young girl of twelve clutching a baby, trying to protect it with her body, he held back from his first impulse to kill them both and tried to allay the fears of the girl who was cowering in the corner of the shelter, knowing that she was going to be killed by the whites. He finally laid down his carbine and held out his arms to the girl and convinced her he meant no harm.

The girl was a beautiful child with a broad face, high cheekbones, almond eyes, and glistening black hair. She was dressed in a buckskin smock with footgear and leggings. The baby belonged to her older sister who had been killed instantly in the first fusillade from the attackers.

When O'Rourke brought the girl and her charge out into the open, a debate immediately commenced about how to dispatch the two of them to their reward. O'Rourke advised everyone that they would have to dispatch him first. "I'll see the first son of a bitch here that raises his hand against this girl and baby in hell before you cut me down."

O'Rourke had established himself as the undisputed head of the miners and, although there were those who would gladly have sent these two "thieving Indians" to their just deserts, none dared challenge the "Big Mick."

After the slaughter at Iron Creek, the miners decided to break their camp and head out of the Gila. They had been terribly disappointed by their prospecting venture and the thought of other Indians lurking nearby to revenge their atrocity spurred them on their way out of the mountains. They had camped on the Gila River before deciding their next move.

When Lilly reached their camp at dusk, she heard about the young Apache girl and baby that were in O'Rourke's charge. Lilly obtained directions to O'Rourke's tent and, as she approached, O'Rourke saw her and arose from cooking his evening meal to greet her, saying in a thick Irish brogue, "Welcome me lady, and what might I be doing fer you this lovely evening?" Patrick had only been in the country for three years and was Irish to the core.

Lilly looked at the handsome Irishman from toe to flaming hair and responded with her own good humor, "They tell me you are a true champion and I would like very much to meet the charges you saved from destruction."

O'Rourke smiled. Here was a woman with the same color of hair as his, firm of mind and body. He thought, without doubt, a child of the Old Sod.

Pat motioned towards the open fly of the tent and said, "Be my guest me lady. Tis an honor to meet a daughter of the Emerald Isle."

Lilly flashed a blazing smile and entered the tent with Patrick right behind. There in the corner sat the beautiful Indian girl, clutching the baby. The child was whimpering. It had been two full days since the miners had surprised the Apache camp and the baby, only six months old, had been without nourishment. The only sustenance it had received was water it had sucked from a dampened rag.

In one look, Lilly could tell from the sallow complexion of

the child that it was in real trouble and needed milk immediately. It was obviously too young to take any solid food and Lilly turned to Pat and said, "This child is going to die if it doesn't receive milk. I can push on tonight and take it to Silver City. Otherwise, it will surely die."

Patrick responded, "Praise the saints, you are an angel, lady. I know that's right, and if you have room for my worthless self, I'll accompany you to protect you on your trip."

The Apache girl had stared in wonderment as this beautiful person entered the tent. She didn't understand a word that was being said but she instinctively knew that the woman was there to help her and save the baby's life. The girl's Apache name was "Morning Mist" and she mirrored such haunting beauty.

Lilly looked at the big Irishman, fascinated by his obvious physical power, and yet so poetic and sensitive in speech. She replied, "I could not ask for a better champion."

On the spot, Patrick O'Rourke sold his two burros, his tent, and his pack to fellow Irishman, Patrick Haggerty, and accompanied Lilly to her buggy. This venture was not viewed with any acclaim by the other miners as their brush with the Indians had convinced them that the Indian menace was all about and they didn't want to loose O'Rourke. They were also haunted by the prospect of Indian revenge.

Haggerty desperately tried to talk his friend and this beautiful woman from embarking on such a hostile adventure, saying, "Patrick, me boy, surely you realize that this is a foolish thing you do. You are only risking your life and the life of this lovely colleen, and these Indian children that you wish to save."

To which O'Rourke replied, "Patrick, you have the burros at one-tenth their price and my tent at even less, the supplies are free. Go with God, me lad, and make a fortune for both of us. As for me, I'm determined to saves these lives that I now am responsible for."

Patrick, of course, was referring to an Irish tradition that if you saved a life, you became responsible for it and until your dying day had to protect and defend the one you had saved from death.

Patrick O'Rourke had the reigns as they pulled out of the miners' camp, heading towards Silver City. The moon had just risen full in the east and the road was easy to follow, well defined by the constant travel between the mining communities. They slipped through the night at a quick trot while Lilly attempted to allay the fears of the young Indian girl by putting her shawl around her and holding her close and comforting her and the clinging baby.

It was near midnight when they reached the Ryan Ranch about halfway to Silver City where they stopped and exchanged horses. More importantly, there was milk available to give the baby by sopping it in the cloth that the young Apache girl still clutched. The baby responded immediately, and suckled as much of the nourishment as it could. When they left the Ryan Ranch, they took a jar of milk which Morning Mist continued to give suckle to her niece as they rode along.

It was an hour after dawn when they reached Silver City, driving directly to the hospital which had been established next to the stage station.

A miner had been bitten by a rabid coyote and, by chance, a doctor was still on duty tending to the poor man who had been lashed to a bed in his deliriums. By fortunate chance, there were three women in the hospital who had given birth to children and were suckling them. The Apache baby was soon contentedly ingesting real mother's milk.

Lilly, by signs, persuaded the young girl to leave the baby there where it could be cared for and go with her to the hotel. Morning Mist was terrified. And yet she knew this beautiful apparition was helping her. And she also knew that the child was responding to the warm milk it was receiving.

It was a strange sight when Lilly checked into the hotel with the Indian girl in her native garb and the big redheaded Irishman with her. She signed up for two rooms. That night Lilly slept with the Indian girl, holding her gently in her arms. She took Morning Mist's hands in hers and guided them to her distant belly so that she could feel the stirring life within. This intimate sharing of the unborn child eased the fear Morning Mist had of her benefactor. Morning Mist had been eleven years old when the final contest between the whites and the Warm Springs had started. Her mother and father and many other relatives had been killed in the constant warfare. Her only brother was Tis-ta-dae, a follower of Nana, who was on campaign fighting the whites.

The morning of the attack by the miners, the Apaches had been camped waiting for Nana and his braves to return from Mexico. The men with them were warriors who were wounded and, needing rest, had been left behind to guard the women and children while the other men were in the field.

It was late in the afternoon when Lilly finally awoke and found the Apache girl already dressed standing by the window, looking out on the streets of Silver City. Lilly quickly dressed and the two of them went down to the hotel restaurant where Lilly ordered a meal for them. Morning Mist was totally unfamiliar with everything she ate, but she was very hungry by this time and anxious to see her niece. Her instincts told her where they were next going. After the meal, Lilly called for her buggy and they went to the hospital where they visited the baby who was responding by leaps and bounds.

While Lilly was hurrying to Silver City to save the life of the Indian infant, the three warriors, and one woman who had escaped the slaughter by the miners had met up with Nana's band returning from Mexico. They told the horrible story of the battle at Iron Creek and the loss of everyone. Tis-ta-dae was devastated to learn of the death of his two sisters and niece. The mate of the older girl had been killed only a month earlier in a battle with Mexican troops south of El Paso. Tis-ta-dae was seeing his family disintegrate but there was no other choice as the whites gave no quarter, would permit no Indian presence where Indian land held the promise of treasure.

The day after arriving in Silver City, Lilly rented a house and moved in to await her own confinement. She hired O'Rourke to stay with her as a guard and also to allay the fear of Morning Mist, who recognized him as her savior. Next, Lilly hired one of the ladies at the hospital who had been suckling the Indian child to move into the house also. The woman's husband was a miner who had been killed in a cave-in just to the north of Silver City when a shaft had collapsed.

Ten days later, Lilly went into labor and gave birth to a son she named Jason. After two weeks of recovery, Lilly was ready to return to Mogollon. This time she bought an extra buggy and team to transport the entire party, which consisted of her, the two Indian children, Patrick O'Rourke, and Mrs. McClusky, the wet nurse, and Mrs. McClusky's children.

It took three days for Lilly's party to return to Mogollon and she immediately set about creating a different environment for her Apache charges and her new son. She commissioned O'Rourke to go into the countryside and begin to purchase as many of the small ranches as he could to create a land base for Lilly to pass on to her charges.

O'Rourke appeared to most people to be an affable giant who had no sensitivity but, in reality, he was a shrewd, calculating businessman and, for the first time in his life, he had been set upon a task worthy of his talent. Within a year he had assembled some sixteen individual ranches into a giant cattle barony, with O'Rourke as patron. For years, he would run this empire, adding to it consistently, and developing and improving the range and the quality of the cattle that Lilly owned.

Just west of the crossing of the Gila River, Lilly commenced a headquarters which would be unequaled in the Southwest. The architecture was Territorial Spanish and the grandeur and majesty was monumental.

Banker Wilson had a keen eye for a profit and kept the business ventures that he and Lilly shared on target. Lilly, on the other hand, had a more compassionate attitude and was constantly partnering with and befriending the miners and other adventurers who came to Mogollon and, over a period of time, became a part of almost every activity carried on in the community and its environs. While Banker Wilson made a handsome profit, Lilly struck a miraculous bonanza and became a partner in many of the most successful mines in the region. Coincidentally, as O'Rourke put together her ranching interests, she amassed a significant fortune in minerals.

CHAPTER FIFTEEN

RESCUE

In the Spring of 1880, Nana and fifteen braves rendezvoused with Victorio at the Meadows in the heart of the Gila. Nana and his group had just returned from raiding deep into Mexico, coming out through the town of Janos and passing near Columbus before reaching the sanctuary of the Gila. Victorio's group had been further to the east raiding in the state of Chihuahua.

Both groups were loaded with plunder including horses, gold, and captives. The captives were young boys and teenage girls. The boys would be given an opportunity to become Apaches and the girls were intended for camp work and marriage. The two groups would have been jubilant at being together and sharing great victories but for the chilling news they received from survivors of the raid by the miners of Iron Creek. The death of so many Warm Springs was calamitous.

Tis-ta-dae was hard hit to lose both of his sisters and a niece. That night around the campfires, many a vow was taken to avenge this savage taking of the lives of women and children. Tis-ta-dae went off by himself and climbed a low bench where earlier he had spent many an hour contemplating and reflecting the fate of his people when he had been at the meadows recovering from severe wounds received at the battle of Camp Sherman. Tis-ta-dae stayed there until the moon was high, trying to understand the nature of the white man who tolerated no culture other than his own and who seemed bent on destroying the last vestige of the Warm Springs Apache Tribe.

The next day, Tis-ta-dae grilled the survivors of the massacre about the fate of his family. The Indians told him that they had returned to the site of their camp after the miners had left to tend to the dead. They had found the body of Tis-ta-dae's older sister in front of the wickiup but they could not find the body of the younger sister and the niece.

Tis-ta-dae pressed them hard as to whether or not they might have been captured and might be alive, or whether they had fled into the forest. The two Indians had no idea which might be the case or whether they were lying dead somewhere, hidden in a crack or crevice of the battlefield area. They had not tarried long in their duties for fear the whites might return.

The Apaches remained camped at the Meadows for three weeks and then planned a departure. It was dangerous to stay in one place too long for fear of discovery and subsequent ambush. During this time, a few Apaches joined the group.

They were individual stragglers, except in one case where three braves came in together. They were Chiricahua Apaches who had been fighting alongside Geronimo in Mexico. They had been cut off from the border and struck out for the Meadows in hopes of finding some of the Warm Springs camped there or near by. One of the Chiricahuas was a cousin of Tis-ta-dae. By stroke of luck, they had news of two Apache captives at Mogollon which stirred hope in Tis-ta-dae's heart for the safety of his relatives.

A group of Geronimo's warriors, including the two Chiricahuas, had captured a Mexican two weeks earlier who had been a captive of the Apaches when he was a young boy. He spoke the language fluently and was a treasure-trove of information. One of the things he told them was that he had driven some beeves to Mogollon for sale and saw two Apaches living with the woman who owned the restaurant and saloon. They were girls. One of them being but an infant. He did not know how they had been captured or any other explicit details that would give a clue to their identities. But Tis-ta-dae was convinced in his heart that this had to be his baby sister and the daughter of his other sister.

Tis-ta-dae asked Nana's permission to make a rescue effort for the two Apache captives with a couple of volunteers to help him. Nana was upset that his trusted lieutenant would want to do something so foolish for personal reasons. He pointed out, "It is a foolhardy to make a raid into the heart of the white's stronghold where there are so many heavily armed men and a detachment of cavalry."

Tis-ta-dae begged for just five days to make the effort and promised he would abandon it at that time if not successful and join Nana in Dog Canyon, the site of their next rendezvous. Nana relented and gave his consent, after all, Tis-ta-dae was truly his right arm. Even though he disapproved of the purpose of the mission, felt compelled to grant Tis-ts-dae this request that meant so much.

When Tis-ta-dae asked for volunteers, the hands of every Apache brave who heard his request went into the air. Tis-ta-dae selected Chubasco and another friend, Net-sen-hey, to accompany him. They quickly made their preparations, assembling weapons, jerky, pemmican, and light sleeping rolls in which were stashed extra moccasins.

By the middle of the afternoon of the second day they were perched on a height overlooking Mogollon where they waited for the sun to set. Tis-ta-dae could see the saloon and restaurant on the north edge of town where he had been told the captives were being kept. When night fell, the three warriors approached Mogollon, circling it from the north and, by midnight, were at the back of the restaurant.

Tis-ta-dae cautiously peeked in a window and saw two people doing the dishes by kerosine lantern. There was, however, no sign of a red headed woman or Apache captives. Tis-ta-dae was beginning to wonder about the reliability of the information given him by the two Chiricahuas and was turning to leave when a noise caused him to look back. He saw a redheaded woman in a long robe enter the kitchen carrying a lantern. Lilly had come in from a door to the south which connected to her living quarters. The woman spoke briefly to the two kitchen workers and then went back through the door. Tis-ta-dae was certain that this was the lady the Mexican captives had seen with the Apache children.

The Indians conferred with each other and decided that it was best to wait for a while as Chubasco, in reconnoitering the building, had determined that there were four or five men still in the saloon on the front side. Chubasco continued to watch the front of the building and reported when the men had all left. He didn't realize that Alfonse, Lilly's husband and the saloon manager, was still inside cleaning up. Since the kitchen workers had gone to bed, the Apaches decided it would be safe to enter the building and search for the Apache captives.

One of the kitchen windows had not been locked, providing an easy entrance. The Apaches, resolute fighters in the outdoors, were very uneasy in these unfamiliar surroundings. Tis-ta-dae had only been in a white man's structure on a few occasions and had no idea how to make his search, other than go through the door where the woman had made her entrance and departure.

The kitchen was dimly lit by moonlight and the Apaches could barely see to make their way across the room. They slowly opened the door which led from the kitchen to Lilly's personal quarters. They found themselves in a sitting room and a search revealed no Apaches or anyone else present.

There were two doors leading off the sitting room and Tis-ta-dae decided to try the left-hand one first. He pushed on the door and then he pulled, but nothing happened. Then he discovered that the handle he was holding could turn. When he turned it, he could hear a latch moving and suddenly the door was free to move. The door opened into the other room and slowly Tis-ta-dae and his two companions entered.

By the dim light, Tis-ta-dae could see the outline of a bed in the far side of the room. He made his way slowly to the bed and, looking down, could see the outline of the woman who he had seen in the kitchen. She seemed to be asleep. She actually was very wide awake having heard the movement of the latch and, through eyes almost closed, she could see the outline of someone standing over the bed. She had no idea who it might be and chose to lay motionless until a course of action became clear.

Tis-ta-dae then moved to his left where he had seen the outline of another bed. In this bed was his sister, sound asleep. The other two braves were waiting in the center of the room for Tis-ta-dae to signal what they should do. When Tis-ta-dae moved towards the other bed, Lilly sprang from her own bed and raced across the room to reach a revolver that was laying on a bureau top. She didn't reach the gun and, instead, ran directly into the arms of Chubasco, who restrained her. In the process, a table was knocked over and Lilly got out a healthy cry for help before her mouth was smothered by Chubasco's hand. Alfonse was just leaving the front door for the night when he heard the commotion and the cry for help from Lilly. In response, he bailed across the room and burst through the door to Lilly's bedroom. Net-sen-hey heard the man coming and as he came through the door Alfonse met Net-sen-hey's knife as it plunged to it's hilt in his chest. There was still fight left in Alfonse, however, and he struggled with Net-sen-hey for a few seconds before his ruptured heart stilled.

The restaurant help had gone to bed upstairs and did not hear any of the ruckus taking place in Lilly's quarters. Tis-ta-dae's sister, however, had awakened immediately and called out in Apache, "Who is there?"

Tis-ta-dae answered, "It is I, Tis-ta-dae." And a joyful reunion resulted.

Lilly could see that the intruder was someone known to her ward, Morning Mist, and felt some relief as a result. Perhaps they would not all be killed after all. In the excitement, she did not know that Alfonse had been struck down and was lying dead on the floor.

Tis-ta-dae asked his sister if the niece was alive and she told him, "Yes, she was in the cradle the other side of Lilly's bed, along with Lilly's own son." Tis-ta-dae walked over and could see the two children in the cradle sleeping, side by side in spite of all the noise. Tis-ta-dae ordered his sister to get the baby and they were going to clear out immediately.

Morning Mist protested this decision and told Tis-ta-dae that the baby could not survive, that there was a woman upstairs who was nursing her and that there was no way the baby could live without a supply of milk. Tis-ta-dae told his sister that no matter, they would be in Dog Canyon in three days and there would be some woman there with child who could take care of the little girl. Morning Mist still protested and said, "The baby will not live that long. I will go willingly, but not the baby."

She added, "This woman has been wonderful to us, and she should not be harmed in any way."

Tis-ta-dae conferred with his friends and they reluctantly agreed that it would be difficult to nourish the infant adequately while they caught up with the rest of the Apache force.

Tis-ta-dae had learned in the heat of battle to make quick decisions and stick to them. He agreed with his sister that the child could stay and they quickly, on his orders, tied up Lilly, gagging her securely. They then left the building through the same window they had entered and circled back to the north and made their escape through the heart of the roughest terrain in the Gila, joining up with Nana and Victorio three days later in Dog Canyon.

Lilly remained bound and gagged throughout the night, lying on the floor next to Alfonse. She couldn't move enough to extricate herself from the bonds or to get out of the room but she did manage to wiggle far enough towards the door to encounter the body of Alfonse. She was horrified when her senses finally told her that this was her dead husband lying beside her.

Lilly was confronted with two great tragedies at the same time. Her ward, Morning Mist, who she had come to love as her own child, abducted by wild Apaches, and Alfonse, her trusted friend, lying dead in a pool of blood because he had come to her aid.

Lilly spent the rest of the night slowly inching her way into the saloon and was at the bottom of the staircase when the breakfast cook came down to get the kitchen started.

As the cook was untying Lilly, Mrs. McCluskey, the wet maid, made an appearance and Lilly told her to check on the baby. They could hear a squall coming from the other room and it was obvious that the baby was still there. When Mrs. McCluskey entered the room and saw the dead body of Alfonse she screamed and fainted. All of the commotion awakened the other kitchen help and they came pouring down to find out what the matter was.

Lilly was hysterical and screaming, demanding that they get the doctor and the Marshal. One of the dishwashers raced down the street, first stopping at the Marshal's Office to tell Joe Doyle who was having his morning coffee, "There was a massacre in the saloon."

He then raced another half-block and climbed a flight of outside stairs to the doctor's office bursting in on the Doctor and his first patient of the day with the same message. Marshal Doyle ran as fast as he could the two blocks to the saloon and was panting heavily when he finally reached Lilly's side.

Lilly, by now, was in a state of total shock, having spent five hours gagged and bound tightly, fearing that Alfonse was dead and desperately trying to free herself and alert someone to the tragedy that had occurred. Doctor Blake came into the room and quickly gave Lilly a double dose of laudanum before he examined Alfonse.

A glance at the body told him what he was going to find. The pool of blood in which the body lay was the size of a cowhide spread on the floor. Doctor Blake directed that Lilly be taken upstairs and that someone stay with her until the shock of everything had worn thin. In the meantime, the undertaker arrived to carry Alfonse back to his mortuary.

Marshal Doyle organized a posse to carry out Lilly's passionate plea to find Morning Mist. It was easy to tell from the tracks that Indians were the perpetrators of this nights work. Word spread throughout the town that Victorio's entire force had attacked Mogollon during the night. The posse followed the tracks back to where the horses had been tied and then northward, swinging around the town itself for about three miles before the tracks were lost in a rock slide.

Doyle knew there was no hope of catching up with the Indians who were the masters of the rim and reluctantly ordered the posse back to town. Later on that afternoon he visited Lilly who had returned to rationality and told her, "It is impossible to find the trail of the Indians."

He speculated, "The raid must have been intended fo find and recover the girl. Not one thing had been taken and there had been no effort to kill Lilly. Killing Alfonse is something they did as a result of his intrusion. If they weren't after guns, provisions, or victims, they had to be after Morning Mist and Nakita."

Lilly and Doyle did not know that the leader of the Indians making this bold foray was Tis-ta-dae who had participated in the attack on the corrals at Camp Sherman.

Lilly grieved at the great loss she had suffered, but had some consolation in that the life of both babies had been spared and that their destiny was in her hands.

The raid on Mogollon was reported in newspapers as far away as New York and served to fan the flames of hatred and prejudice towards the "bestial Apache." Speeches were made on the floor of Congress that this Apache scourge had to be dealt with immediately and firmly. The Army was reeling under pressure because of its inability to contain the Warm Springs uprising. Now they were being ridiculed by the press and citizens. Lilly's protector, Patrick O'Rourke, had been out of town the night of the raid by Tis-ta-dae. He was overseeing the building of an extensive ranch house at the Gila crossing. Lilly believed that the boom town of Mogollon would someday die and she wanted to establish a firm base for her future and that of her children. She considered the Little Apache child, Nakita, to be as much her child as was Jason.

When O'Rourke heard about the attack, he immediately returned to Mogollon where Lilly insisted that he revise all of the plans to make the new home an impregnable fort against any attack by Indians or others.

The site Lilly had picked was on a low hill overlooking the Gila River and the crossing where she had found Nakita and Morning Mist. The building was built in the style of a Spanish hacienda with an extensive courtyard and thick parapet walls capable of turning even cannon shot. The house was built so that it could be forted up and provide safety even if the outer court fell into hostile hands.

In six months the hacienda was complete and Lilly moved there permanently. She set out to create a ranching business that would provide her and her children with complete security. Banker Wilson's father had been a cattle broker in Chicago and one of Mr. Wilson's brothers was still in the business. There were new

English breeds being introduced into the United States and Wilson's brother highly recommended that they pioneer the use of hereford cattle in the Southwest.

As a result, one day soon after the hacienda had been finished, a cattle train pulled into Silver City with heavy set, red cattle with white faces and short horns. The animals were the butt of many a joke as they trailed out of Silver City on the drive to the Burnt Wagon Ranch. Lilly had named the ranch "Burnt Wagon" in memory of the miners who had befriended her before meeting their deaths at the river crossing.

All of Lilly's friends had warned her not to move to the ranch, that it was isolated and dangerous, and that there was no way to have enough people there to adequately defend it if Victorio or Geronimo decided to move against the sanctuary. Lilly ignored their advice and moved anyway, sensing that the Apaches, in leaving the baby behind, had entrusted her to nourish and protect it. Lilly, wanting to reassure the Apaches that the baby was, in fact, safe, asked Lieutenant Welch in command of a small attachment of Cavalry at Mogollon to instruct his San Carlos Apache scouts to pass the word back to the San Carlos Reservation that the Warm Springs baby was with Lilly at the ranch house she had just built.

Lilly knew from the military that there were some Warm Springs families living on the San Carlos Reservation and she hoped that this news would somehow find its way to the wild Apaches fighting in the mountains.

Six months later word did reach Tis-ta-dae through a San Carlos Warm Springs that his niece was living in the ranch house at the crossing. On the orders of Nana and Victorio, every Apache brave was told that the Burnt Wagon Ranch was not to be disturbed or harassed in any fashion. As a result of the sanctuary provided to Lilly, she was able to continue to acquire neighboring properties and ranch in peace.

While the Burnt Wagon Ranch was a sanctuary, the nearby spreads were not and it was extremely dangerous to be at an isolated ranch headquarters with only a few cowboys with marauding Apaches in the neighborhood.

The Burnt Wagon brand was the circle-bar-circle, representing a wagon bed. Wherever this distinctive brand appeared, Apache depredation did not occur.

CHAPTER SIXTEEN

ABIGAIL VISITS

A week after Lilly had moved into her new ranch home, she received a note delivered by Lieutenant Welch on his way from Mogollon to Fort Bayard. The note was in a precise hand and inquired, "Would you be so kind as to receive me in your new home so that I can make your acquaintance." When Lilly finally got to the signature of the writer, she was dumfounded. The note was signed, "Abigail Wilson." Without doubt, the same Abigail Wilson who had hounded Lilly out of Magdalena four years earlier. In the note Abigail Wilson requested, "Please reply to the Mogollon Hotel." Lilly had no idea why the Banker's wife would be wanting to see her and Lilly mused as to whether Abigail Wilson knew who Lilly really was.

Since leaving Magdalena, Banker Wilson had stayed in touch with his wife through occasional letters, usually two or three a year. He had also made arrangements through the bank in Silver City for her to draft monthly enough to keep her living comfortably. Abigail had written Banker Wilson time and time again, at first demanding that he return at once and then pleading with him to return and save her honor.

When Banker Wilson had left Magdalena, leaving his wife behind, she had explained his absence as a business trip. Many thought when he didn't return that there was some problem with the bank. But, unbeknownst to anyone, Banker Wilson had quietly sold the bank some months before his departure and the new owners had arrived in town by train the day Banker Wilson precipitately left on the stage.

Banker Wilson carried off all of his assets which had been converted to gold bullion and had left enough money with the new owners to provide for his wife until he could relocate himself and send her funds. When it finally became apparent in town that Banker Wilson had deserted his wife, her world crumbled.

It was months before she would even show her face outside the front door.

After four years, she had finally decided the time had come for a showdown, so she swallowed the last vestige of pride and came to Mogollon in spite of the hazards of travel to plead with her husband to let her join him. Her entreaties fell on deaf ears. She had made his life hell for twenty years and he was deliriously happy being separated from her. He offered to provide her with additional funds to locate her anywhere she wanted and said he would continue to assist her financially. He did not propose divorce but absolutely refused reconciliation. Abigail saw him daily, pleading her case to no avail.

She had inquired of the hotel keeper's wife about the social life of Mogollon and had been told there was a very wealthy woman who was the arbiter of all society in that region of New Mexico, referring, of course, to Lilly. The hotel keeper's wife had no knowledge of Lilly's business activities on the hill and, as a result, Abigail Wilson set a trap for herself in making the request for an audience.

Lilly wrote that she would love to see the visitor and suggested that she come to the ranch at her convenience.

Banker Wilson finally convinced his wife that there was no possible reunion and she finally accepted his offer of a carriage and driver to take her to Silver City. She had decided to return to Chicago where her father still lived but wanted to at least establish her social ranking in the area by visiting the universally acknowledged arbiter of gentility.

And so it was with Abigail's great expectation that the buggy turned off the main road, up the driveway and through the imposing gates of the courtyard of Burnt Wagon Ranch.

Abigail was impressed with the size of the house and the opulence of everything within view. She pulled back the ponderous knocker and waited to be admitted into the most beautiful home she had ever seen. The massive door was opened by a gigantic redheaded Irishman who introduced himself to Mrs. Wilson as Patrick O'Rourke. Abigail gave O'Rourke her card and he sent it upstairs to Lilly by one of the maids. Lilly had the girl come back down and tell her guest that it would be a little while but she would be down. Lilly was, in fact, feverishly putting on her finest dress and loading up on jewelry. Lilly was not a vain person, very disciplined to not show off or be ostentatious, but this was one time she was going to bust a gut to be as grandiose as possible.

Finally, Lilly was ready and came down the staircase to the parlor where the maid had left Abigail Wilson. Lilly walked into the room absolutely glittering. She was thirty years old and at the very peak of her physical attraction. Lilly walked over to where Mrs. Wilson was sitting and, when Mrs. Wilson stood up, extended her hand and said, "How nice to see you, Mrs. Wilson."

Mrs. Wilson replied, "Thank you very much for permitting me to visit. How lovely you are my dear. But don't we know each other?" The two women stood there for a moment looking at one another, one of them typifying everything that was outward and visible, and the other typifying everything that was inward and hidden.

Lilly answered Mrs. Wilson's question saying, "I don't believe we have ever met, but I certainly know who you are."

It was true that they had never met. They had seen each other on the streets of Magdalena but Banker Wilson's wife would never have shaken the hand or engaged in conversation with a barroom girl. Yet here she was doing exactly that, and in great awe.

In four years, Lilly had matured into a beautiful woman with great poise and charm. Abigail immediately began to babble about her important husband, Banker Wilson, and how he wanted her to stay with him in Mogollon so much that it was breaking his heart for her to leave, but she had to go back to Chicago to be with her aged father. And, of course, there were so many social attractions there that she would be kept so busy, and on and on she went trying to impress this beautiful and wealthy creature with how important a guest she had in her home.

Lilly let her continue on interminably, wanting desperately to interrupt her and blurt out, "Hey, I'm Lilly, the bar girl you ran out of Magdalena, what do you think of me now, sister?"

But she couldn't bear to do it, seeing how desperately Mrs.

Wilson was trying to put on a good face and play the role of a Chicago socialite married to a wealthy Southwestern entrepreneur. Abigail talked so incessantly that the afternoon had almost waned when she said she better be going on. Lilly insisted that it was far too late to start towards Silver City and insisted that she spend the night. Abigail was very willing to assent to the offer of shelter and Lilly sent one of the servants to attend to the driver who had brought Mrs. Wilson to the ranch.

That evening, the two ladies had dinner with O'Rourke and the tirade continued. O'Rourke, of course, did not know all of the background of the previous relationship of the women, but did know that everything Abigail was handing out about her relationship with Banker Wilson was a bunch of blarney. He was amused at what she was saying and realized without being told that here was a bitter, mean spirited, disappointed woman who had been cast aside and was trying to play the part of queen bee.

After a couple of glasses of wine, Abigail was even more loquacious and it was with great relief that she finally announced to her two dinner mates, "I'm just exhausted from my journey, do you mind if I retire?"

Lilly escorted Abigail to her room and, once again, before saying goodnight, Abigail insisted, "Haven't we met?"

Lilly assured her, "We have never been introduced."

Lilly went back downstairs and O'Rourke was carrying the wine bottle back to the liquor pantry when Lilly suggested he find a bottle of Brandy so that they could have a nightcap together. She laughingly said, "Don't you think we deserve some reward?"

O'Rourke smiled and said, "My dear, your presence made up for any discomfort, but it's a bright idea you have."

Patrick returned with a bottle of aged brandy, which Lilly had ordered from Spain, and when O'Rourke pulled the chair back for her to sit down at the dining room table, she looked at him and said, "We would be more comfortable in my room."

She turned and walked to the stairs. O'Rourke knew from her look and words that she wanted his company that night and he gladly followed her up the stairway.

He did not know why he had stumbled onto such good fortune but, whatever it was, no questions were going to be asked. As for Lilly, she did not know why the impulse had overcome her to spend the evening with O'Rourke. She had not been with anybody since her assignation with Lieutenant Whiting and her pent up ardor needed cooling; but she was also consciously doing it on purpose, because under the same roof slept the woman whose own cold spite and hate had driven her out of Magdalena into the world of wealth and comfort she now enjoyed. Whatever the reason, Lilly was a very happy and contented woman when the morning sun streamed in her window tinting her complexion and radiantly reflecting from her hair.

She glanced to her side to see if O'Rourke was there and found that he had already arisen. As the ranch foreman, he was a very busy man as 15,000 head of cattle were now grazing on the Burnt Wagon spread.

Not long after Lilly had gone downstairs and started the cooks on their breakfast chores, Abigail made her appearance again profusely discussing her pedigree and culture and her terrible shame at leaving her husband behind while she went to the glitter and excitement of Chicago. Lilly listened and smiled and replied with the etiquette necessary and finally stood on the front veranda bidding her guest good-bye while once again Abigail asked, "I am just positive we have known each other some place before."

At that moment, O'Rourke came up , aid, "Good-bye," to Abigail and assisted her into her carriage. Lilly was spared another white lie.

The driver flipped the whip and the double team pulled out, heading for Silver City. As the buggy left, Lilly thought to herself that she would never see Abigail again. She knew only too well how Banker Wilson felt about his estranged wife and, to her surprise, she felt sorry for the woman and wished there was something she might do to ease the burden of Abigail's guilt.

When the buggy reached the main road and turned left towards Silver City, Abigail thought of how nice Lilly had been and that it was very important that she continue to correspond with her after she had reached Chicago surely her husband will shortly ask her to join him and it will be very important to be socially aligned with the most famous woman in the territory. Abigail was now, herself, convinced that she had never met Lilly, but was still trying to recall who it was that Lilly reminded her of as the horses patiently trotted toward Silver City.

CHAPTER SEVENTEEN — JASON KIDNAPPED

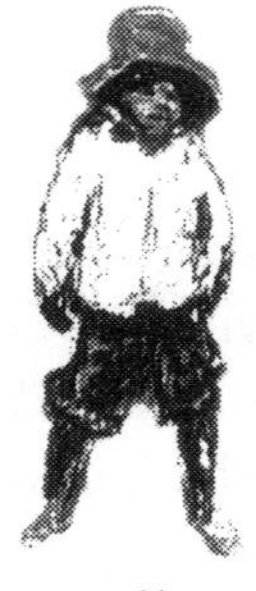

After Mrs. Wilson's visit, Lilly got in the habit of inviting her foreman, O'Rourke, to her bedroom once or twice a week. While he was a big, vigorous, macho man in his dealings with the ranch hands and others, with Lilly he was a kind and gentle person, very solicitous of her moods and vicissitudes. She soon got to the point where she counted on his companionship and when he, one evening while tenderly embracing her, asked her to marry him, she said, "Yes!"

From Lilly's point of view no better a husband could ever have lived. He was attentive, tuned into her every mood. The next four years were happy for Lilly. Both she and Wilson had sold their interests in the two "painted lady" houses on top of the hill to Lupe.

Lilly sold the saloon, hotel and restaurant for a fair price, but on gracious terms, to O'Rourke's old friend Haggerty who had hit pay dirt on Nickel Creek above Mogollon.

Everyone in the area was delighted at the marriage of Lilly and O'Rourke. Even Doyle was pleased to see the two so happy but at the same time was bitterly envious. He still loved Lilly. He had ever since they had been on the stage together from Magdalena to Silver City. He had watched her love for Lieutenant Whiting develop on the stage ride, and from her confession, knew that he had fathered her son. He was jealous of Alfonse, because he had wanted to make that pleasant sacrifice. Now that she had married O'Rourke, it seemed that he had been passed up for all time. Lilly was thirty-four and Marshal Doyle was fifty-five. It looked like he was headed for permanent bachelorhood.

The Marshal had a girlfriend now and then but there never was anyone in his life who fired his passion as did Lilly. He frequently found himself awakening at night fantasizing about Lilly and this bothered him greatly as he prided his ability to control his emotions and be dispassionate. A lawman who is emotional, doesn't stay alive. You had to fire your gun and make your moves with your head, not your heart.

O'Rourke, on the other hand, at forty, settled into an idealistic life that he dared not dream about before. While his wife was wealthy, he was providing his own significant contribution, the best management any spread could possibly have. He was the ideal father to Lilly's son, Jason, and cherished the little Indian girl, Nakita, as if they were both offspring of his loins.

Their ideal life lasted for two years and then tragedy struck.

There was a big cattle drive taking the year's crop of calves to Silver City for shipment by rail to the eastern markets. Three days after the cattle drive had begun, O'Rourke and Lilly's son, Jason, started out by buggy to catch up with the herd to oversee the bargaining with the cattle buyers. No one gave a thought to Apache depredations as Victorio had been slain in Mexico and the bands under Geronimo and Juh were confined to Old Mexico except for occasional raids into the close border areas. There had been no activity in the Gila for almost two years and everyone had breathed a sigh of relief, feeling that the danger was past.

A Navajo who had been fighting alongside Geronimo in Old Mexico had decided he wanted to see his family and had talked two apostate Mexicans and two Netdahe Apaches into making the trip with him to the Alamosa Reservation. They crossed the desert undetected and slipped through the Gila and finally reached the Navajo reservation at Alamosa.

These wild Indians appearing without notice at the reservation caused quite a stir. Fearful that some of the Navajos would disclose their presence, they left on the second day. The Indian agent at Alamosa, although he had been told there were some wild Indians from Mexico on the reservation, had not believed it and, as a result, there was no alarm given concerning the presence of hostiles.

The group passed through the Gila on their return without event and were in sight of the Silver City road when they saw a buggy coming along the side of Mangas Creek. The raiders hid themselves in a clump of scrub oak along the road and, as the buggy pulled abreast, they suddenly appeared and opened fire.

They were on the left-hand side of the road and O'Rourke was in the left side of the buggy. As a result, every bullet found its mark in O'Rourke and jolted his body to the right, falling over and covering young Jason. With the first fusillade, the horses broke into a dead run and it was five minutes before one of the Netdahes was able to reach the reins and pull the horses in. The Indians were sorely disappointed. There was no bootie, no money, nothing; some papers in a valise, a gun, and that was it. They had to be content with the horses as the buggy was of no use to them.

They unhooked the horses and debated what to do with the young boy who cowered on the floorboards of the buggy. Finally, they decided to take him along to the stronghold in the Sierra Madre. Young boys were always good to assign camp duties to and they often grew up to become outstanding warriors. One of the renegades in the band had been a captive and he had argued forcefully to spare young Jason's life and take him back with them.

O'Rourke's lifeless body laid on the seat of the buggy for two days before the first traveler came along and discovered the tragedy. Lilly was devastated at the news. Just when her life seemed to have taken on real meaning and purpose. She was deeply in love with a good man. The joy of raising a son and the satisfaction of having Nakita, whom she had adopted as her child, gave her all of the contentment a mother feels as she molds her children.

When the news arrived, Lilly gathered every hand on the ranch and immediately set off on horseback with them to the scene of the slaying. It had not rained since the day of the tragedy and it was obvious from the tracks that the hostiles had taken off towards Mexico. Lilly and her men raced for three days and three nights, now and then catching a sign of the trail, until they arrived at Lordsburg with all traces of the trail gone. It was obvious, though, that they were heading for Mexico and the last Apache stronghold deep in the heart of the Sierra Madre. Reluctantly, Lilly was convinced to give up the chase and return to the Burnt Wagon Ranch, but not without first posting a reward for ten thousand dollars for information about the whereabouts of her son.

CHAPTER EIGHTEEN  THE STRONGHOLD

Lilly attended to a few ranch matters and then, leaving everything in charge of O'Rourke's top hand, journeyed to Mogollon. She checked into the hotel and sought out Marshal Doyle knowing that he was the one man in the Southwest who could find a way to rescue her son. Joe had heard the terrible news and was not surprised when Lilly showed up seeking his aid.

By chance, two days earlier, a cavalry detachment working south of Mogollon had come across two Warm Springs Indians who had slipped away from Geronimo's camp and were heading for the San Carlos Reservation to join their families. The cavalry would frequently leave Indian prisoners with Marshal Doyle while they arranged for their transportation to other places. Doyle told Lilly that he had two Warm Springs who might be able to help them. Neither one of them spoke English but there was a San Carlos interpreter with the cavalry troop stationed at Mogollon.

Marshal Doyle asked the young officer in charge to release the two Warm Springs and the San Carlos interpreter to his custody as a U.S. Marshal to assist in recovering Jason. The Lieutenant knew he was on thin ice and asked Doyle, "Will you put that in writing as an order?" When Doyle assented, he released the prisoners and one of his scouts.

The two Warm Springs had tired of the incessant warfare and separation of the families. They were happy to agree to help Lilly in her mission, thinking that it would bring them great favor with the army troops and perhaps lead to favored treatment. They were also terrified at the prospect of exile or hanging which was frequently mentioned among the Apaches as the punishment they could expect to find after twice breaking from San Carlos.

It was obviously crucial that the party had to be as small as possible and so it was only Lilly and Marshal Doyle and the three Indians who left Mogollon on their way to the Apache stronghold in Mexico.

They rode southwest, passing north of Lordsburg, striking the Chiricahua Mountains on the fourth day. They circled the eastern side of the Chiricahuas and then headed southwest towards the river Bavispe where the two Warm Springs said the main camp of the Indians would be found. Three days later they were deep into the Sierra Madre and an eerie silence had descended upon them. They saw no game, they heard no birds calling. It was as if death were everywhere.

Through the San Carlos interpreter they had been told that the Apache holdouts had killed all the game in the area and that this was one of the reasons they were considering suing for peace. It was becoming impossible to raid because of the vigilance of the Mexican and American cavalries and there was no way to maintain their numbers off the bounty of the land.

On the fourth day, they reached a deep canyon which they were told led to the Bavispe. Here the guides stopped and set up camp, saying that the hostiles would contact them when they were ready. They had been in view for two days.

As predicted, that afternoon an Apache entered camp first calling out his name and verifying the identity of the two Warm Spring guides. He came in and sat down and asked for tobacco, which Marshal Doyle had brought along. He seemed very relaxed and unconcerned about the penetration of whites so deep into their domain. This was because talk of surrender had been going on for two weeks. Geronimo was of a mind to call it quits and to lay down his arms while the Netdahe were arguing to hold out forever if need be.

The two groups were of even numbers and it appeared from time to time that a fight might break out between them over the issue of surrender. The Netdahes saw things differently from the Warm Springs because they had their wives and children with them. The Warm Springs Bednokohes and Chiricahuas had many relatives at the San Carlos Reservation who they missed dearly.

The Apache who had made contact with them, after learning the purpose of their mission, told them to wait there while he went back to receive instructions. The following day he returned and told them that it was all right to come on, but that the San

Carlos interpreter must remain behind.

Before leaving camp, Lilly and Marshal Doyle were both blindfolded, and their hands were tied behind them. It was difficult to stay on the horses riding up the steep trail even though the animals were being led by the Apaches. Both were good riders, though, and managed to stay on their mounts.

Four hours later the blindfolds were removed. They were in the main camp of the Apaches, high above Copper Canyon, overlooking a panorama of forest crests cut by deep canyons, the most spectacular and awesome landscape in the world. They were led into the presence of a council of chiefs sitting in a circle around a fire. The two principal chiefs, sitting at the western end of the circle, were Geronimo and Juh. Next to them were Nana and other Chiefs, including Lozen, the sister of Victorio and Tis-ta-dae, who stood out because of his fierce countenance.

Marshal Doyle advised Lilly that it would be best for him to start the conversation as he wasn't sure how they would accept an assertive woman. Doyle told them, "We come in peace. I have accompanied this woman whose son we believe you have. She wants to talk to you to see if you will return him. She is a good woman and on many occasions has given help to the Apache. I have come along to help her."

He paused surveying his audience and continued, "I am the Marshal at Mogollon and, while I have held your people prisoner, I have treated them with respect and kindness. Ask anyone who has been my prisoner and they will tell you that I have been just and fair. However, I must obey my chief as you obey yours. Thank you for permitting us to come to your council and I ask permission for the lady with me to speak."

Doyle's remarks were translated by a Chiricahua who spoke fair English. Geronimo raised his right hand and said, "We listen. Do you have a message from Nantan Crook," referring to the Army general who had bottled them up in Mexico.

Lilly then stood up and said, "No, we have not come for the army but because of my son who is with you. He was taken prisoner by Apaches eight days ago on the road to Silver City. I own the ranch known as the Burnt Wagon and have befriended your people."

Lilly paused, drawing a deep breath, and continued, "You may know that I have living with me a young Apache girl, Nakita, who survived a terrible attack on your people at Iron Creek. Another Apache girl lived with me until she was taken from me one night in Mogollon by your braves. Surely this young boy can mean nothing to you but to me he means everything."

Lilly's eyes were welling with tears and she had to dab them with her sleeve before finishing. "Please let me have him so that I can take him home. I will do anything you say, pay any price, attempt any task. Thank you for listening to me." Lilly slumped slightly and sat down.

The Chiefs were impressed. Here was a woman who spoke like a man, who minced no words. Geronimo asked Nana to reply and Nana told Lilly, "We understand the reason for you being here. We appreciate that you have been a friend of the Apache. We know you are raising an Apache. We have not bothered you or your ranch."

Nana continued, "The Apaches who took your son attacked without knowing you were under our protection. We are sorry that happened."

Nana paused for a second, and then added, "Do not be concerned. We may not grant your request but we will spare your life."

A heated exchange ensued among the Indians. Juh was opposed to any leniency whatsoever and wanted to kill the Marshal and take the woman as a captive into his own wickiup. The Chiefs from the northern bands and the Chiricahuas argued just as vehemently that this would be a disgrace for the Apache, who should honor decency with decency.

Tis-ta-dae, after listening to the older chiefs, added, "I very much feel that we should grant this woman's wish. I can tell you from talking to my sister that this is a good woman who befriended her and saved the life of my niece and I think that we should save a life for every life that is saved. We should give this woman the life of her son in exchange for the lives she saved."

Tis-ta-dae's speech carried great weight. For him to want leniency was something to respect. Here was the most gifted fighter of all, a brave who had no equal in the number of whites he had killed during the ten years of the Warm Springs uprising.

Juh and the Netdahe were not voted down, they were just ignored by the others and the young boy was sent for. He was brought to the circle by Morning Mist, Tis-ta-dae's sister, who embraced her friend Lilly. Through the Chiricahua interpreter, they spoke to each other and exchanged their vows of love for each other and news of Nakita. Little Jason stayed at his mother's side with her arm around him, in awe of this unbelievable turn of events. He had concluded that his life was over in that savage environment. By some miracle here was his mother, capable of doing anything.

Lilly asked Morning Mist, "Please, if your brother will let you go too, you must come home with me. We miss you terribly. Your niece needs you."

The young girl replied, "No, I can't. I am a woman now and Tis-ta-dae has promised me in marriage to his best friend Chubasco. I am too old to be a child. I must do my duty as an Apache. But I shall always remember you and love you and I know that you will be good to my niece."

The two women embraced, and Morning Mist added, "I just knew this was your son. I don't know how I knew it, but I knew it and I have been very careful to shield him from any harm."

Lilly thanked her profusely and wept openly as she embraced the girl.

The Apache Chiefs were greatly affected. It was obvious that there was a genuine feeling of love and respect between these two women. And tough old Geronimo, with all the callouses on his heart, knew that he had done the right thing. Nana looked approvingly at him and nodded his head, signaling his thanks. Nana knew how much the act of kindness meant to Tis-ta-dae who he saw as his son and alter ego.

The tension that existed at the beginning had totally evaporated and many of the braves were gathering around Marshal Doyle. In particular, they wanted to examine his pistols, the likes of which they had never seen. They were covered with nickel and had beautiful carved white ivory handles. Tis-ta-dae, at this point, noticed that Juh and the Netdahe Chiefs had retired with their men to their side of the camp.

He turned to Nana and motioned him to step away from the group and said, "Thank you uncle for helping me and this lady, but I am afraid we may have a score to settle with our Netdahe friends if we do not get them out of here at once. Look at them over there" pointing at the Netdahe, "they are up to no good."

Coincidentally the great war drum in the Netdahe camp began to sound, thundering across the abyss of Copper Canyon. Nana knew that a few hours of drinking Tesquino would indeed provoke trouble in the Apache camp. He quickly gave orders to the guides to return the whites at once to their camp below. The blindfolds were again applied and a harrowing trip began down the steep slope of the mountain.

Lilly and the Marshal were barely able to stay mounted even though their hands had been freed for the return trip. The boy did much better because he had not been blindfolded and he constantly encouraged his mother and Marshal Doyle to stay on their horses and warned them of dangerous places they had to cross. It was dark when they arrived and they immediately broke camp and started out of the mountain vastness. The two Warm Springs carried a personal and private message from Geronimo to Crook.

CHAPTER NINETEEN  RETURN TO THE U.S.

The moon was bright but low lying clouds made the journey very difficult and their progress was slow as they rode through the night. At dawn, they had reached the northern foothills of the Sierra Madre and were looking for a campsite when they came across a cavalry patrol beginning to break camp. Lilly couldn't believe it, but the patrol leader was Emery Whiting, now a Captain. He was also shocked, even more so than her.

Whiting ordered his men to rest and then helped Lilly dismount. Turning to Marshal Doyle, he said, "Where have you come from? What are you doing here? Don't you know that you are in the heart of the hostile country?"

Joe quickly explained their mission and pointed to Lilly's son at the rear of their little caravan, and said, "We're clearing out of here as quick as we can, and I wouldn't take this little bunch you've got one step further."

Whiting responded, "Geronimo has sent several messages indicating he wants to surrender. We're assigned to a patrol that will take us to Cottonwood Springs where we are to wait for a message from Geronimo."

As they spoke, Whiting kept glancing at Lilly's son, Jason, thinking, My God, is that my child? He looks like me. He looks like me. My God, is it my son?

Lilly and Joe seeing the two together were both struck by the resemblance. Lilly thought, *Is he such a fool that he can't even recognize his own child?* Fool wasn't the way Marshal Doyle characterized Whiting in his mind as he glared at the man who had brought Lilly such unhappiness, thinking, *This worthless son of a bitch can have the world and he is too dumb to even see it. Why should a whimpering, worthless snob have the one thing I can't possess?*

Only the boy was not caught up in this maelstrom of hatred, doubt, and love. Lilly was desperate for some sign from Whiting that he wanted to see her again or talk to her or anything. But Whiting remained reserved and dismissed all thoughts that this could be his child. After all, the evening they had spent together convinced him she was a very experienced woman and the father of that child could be anyone who had ever walked down the streets of Mogollon.

He could not afford to risk his career by marrying a wanton woman. The Army had instilled pride and valor in Whiting but it had failed to make him a man. And while he might distinguish himself for the rest of his career, he failed that day to stand tall and grab for his own what Marshal Doyle would have laid down his life for.

Doyle told Whiting that the two Warm Springs with them had a message for General Crook. Whiting laughed and replied, "Geronimo doesn't know that he must now deal with Miles. He's in for a shock. Miles is no Indian lover."

After a few pleasantries, Whiting announced that he had to move out to keep his rendezvous. The two Warm Springs went with Whiting who gave Doyle a note transferring their custody. Doyle, Lilly, and Jason and their San Carlos guide headed north over the crest of a knoll. As they topped out, Lilly turned in the saddle and, looking back, saw Whiting for the last time, briskly heading south, firmly in the grip of his career.

CHAPTER TWENTY

A PARTY FOR THE MARSHAL

Marshal Joe Doyle propped his feet up on the desk, leaned back in his swivel chair with his hands clasped behind his neck, and settled down for an afternoon snooze. It had been a very quiet day. No emergencies. No calls. There wasn't even a prisoner in the hoosegow requiring attention. It had been a month since the rescue of Jason in Old Mexico.

Geronimo surrendered shortly after the Marshal returned to Mogollon and was promised that the Apaches would be permitted back on their reservation as a term and condition of surrender. He was very suspicious of the good faith of the whites. His doubts and qualms were well founded as, immediately upon surrender, every southern Apache that could be gathered up, man, woman, and child, was sent into exile into Florida.

Such drastic treatment reflected the ferocity and ability with which the southern Apaches defended their homeland. This small group, never numbering more that 450 men in the field at any one time, had held at bay 15,000 American troops, 10,000 Mexican Dragoons, and uncounted numbers of scouts, volunteers, guides, and peace officers.

The Marshal felt bad about the treachery of the American surrender conditions when he heard that all the southern Apache were being loaded on trains and sent to St. Augustine, Florida. He was not surprised, however, as he knew first hand that the Warm Springs had taxed the American army to its limit and they would go to any extreme to be sure that Apaches never again would take the field against them.

The Marshal had been dozing for about a half an hour when the front door opened up. Instantly, the Marshal's eyes were wide open and he could see in the shaving mirror on the west wall that the postmaster was coming in the room. When the Marshal was sitting at his desk, he always had his back to the front door. This was a ruse he had followed for many years. If someone came into the office, bent on mischief, he would think that the Marshal was a sitting duck with his back exposed. The mirror, however, gave the Marshal the advantage as he could clearly see every move of an intruder.

The Marshal had learned this trick from his first job as an Assistant U.S. Marshal in Arkansas under William Polkinghorn. Polkinghorn had taught Doyle all of the tricks of the trade that a lawman needed to know to stay alive and administer frontier justice. Many a time Polkinghorn had lectured young Doyle that a peace officer had to shoot with his head, not his heart, and that the difference between life and death was looking ahead and not behind. A broad back was an inviting target, but it was also one that would lull an attacker into complacency and might give you just the time you needed to gain the advantage.

The postmaster, Stan Roberts, stood looking at the back of Marshal Doyle's head for just a moment and then said, "Joe, you awake? There's a letter here for you from Washington, D.C."

Joe unlimbered his legs from the top of the desk, leaning forward as he swung around, and said, "Let's see what it is, Stan. You don't get many of these, do you?"

The Marshal took an open-bladed knife from the desk drawer and slit the envelope and took out the letter which was from the Chief U.S. Marshal. Joe read the letter with utter amazement. Instead of being chastised for failing to do some job, it was notification of his appointment as Chief U.S. Marshal for the combined territories of Arizona and New Mexico. From the look of shock and disbelief in Doyle's face, Stan could tell that the letter was out of the ordinary.

Not able to contain his curiosity any longer, he stammered out, "Well, well, Marshal what is it? Good or bad?"

The Marshal replied "It is good. It is unbelievable, but it is good. Look at this, Stan, I've been appointed U.S. Marshal for the combined territories of New Mexico and Arizona."

Stan laid down his mailbag and stepped up to the Marshal with his hand held out. Shaking the Marshal's hand, he said, "Joe, it couldn't happen to a better guy. I'm really proud for you."

Joe's face reddened at this praise. While he had a tough reputation and a fierce demeanor, at heart he was very bashful and, of course, appreciative of his friend's kind words. One of the bonuses for living in Mogollon at the time was that the postal service performed the functions of the town crier as well and Stan Roberts did his duty that day. By sundown there wasn't a soul in Mogollon, New Mexico who didn't know about Marshal Joe Doyle's good fortune.

The Marshal couldn't believe it. He had made no move to advance himself. He had been content to do his job and serve out his time and, for the past fifteen years, had been in such out-of-the-way places as Magdalena and Mogollon. The reason for the Marshal's good fortune was the intercession on his behalf by Lilly O'Rourke.

The Marshal's utter disregard for his own personal safety in helping Lilly rescue her son made her determined to somehow pay the good man back. She had taken the stage to Deming where she caught the Southern Pacific into El Paso. There she switched to the Santa Fe and visited the territorial capitol. Tom Catron of the "Santa Fe Ring" had met Lilly on two other occasions and, of course, knew that she had become the wealthiest woman in the territory. He asked Lilly to write out the story of her ordeal and sent it along with his own recommendation directly to President Cleveland.

Lilly's friend, Thadeus Wilson, had left Mogollon, selling all of his holdings and moved to the town of Tucson. Wilson, as one of Arizona's leading citizens, was happy at Lilly's request to add his recommendation to that of many others.

When news of the Marshal's appointment reached Lilly, she was at Burnt Wagon. She had her buggy brought to the front and left for Mogollon to congratulate him. She swept into the Marshal's office and embraced him warmly. As soon as she found out that it would be a week before he had to leave town, she left and rented the saloon for a big party for the Marshal to give everyone in Mogollon a chance to thank him for all he had done for the community for the past ten years.

The party proved to be a real fandango and was talked about in Mogollon for many years after. The only two people who stayed sober were Lilly and the Marshal. Lilly, because she never drank much, and the Marshal because, if he did, he would be a sitting duck for any gun-crazed youth that came along. By good fortune, Banker Wilson was in Mogollon the day of the party, having returned to wind up some of his business matters. The three old friends reminisced that night about their adventures.

Near the close of the evening, the Marshal remarked to Wilson that they might not see each other for a while and he wanted Wilson to know that at one time he actually suspected that Wilson was a crook. The Marshal reminded the Banker that he had carried a carpetbag onto the stage on that ill-fated trip, which he guarded with his life.

The Marshal confided, "I was sure you had stolen something from the bank and you were making a getaway but, when all that Indian problem hit us, I flat forgot to hold you up in Silver City until I could get a search warrant and go through that valise."

Wilson laughed and said, "I guessed that everybody on that stage thought I was absconding with the bank deposits. The truth is, I was leaving with my life savings. I was getting away from the meanest woman who ever lived. I was more afraid of her than death itself and I just snuck out of town when the opportunity presented itself."

The two men laughed and continued to reminisce about all of the things that had happened in the rip-snortin' boomtown of Mogollon during the hectic days of rich strikes, Indian depredations, and the sheer risk of being alive on the Mogollon Rim.

The highlight of the evening was the presentation to Marshal Doyle of a present from all of the townspeople. It was a massive mineral specimen with quartz crystals the size of quarters and a gold seam running from end to end a quarter of an inch wide. It had come from one of the glory holes found north of Mogollon and was worth several thousand dollars in gold content alone. As a mineral specimen, it was unique in the world. Marshal Doyle deserved a handsome present, he had served Mogollon well. He had kept the peace, settled disputes, and been at the forefront of every community effort on behalf of the town.

It was 2:00 a.m. when the last reveler left the North Star

Saloon, so tipsy that he needed two fellow celebrants to support him from each side. It's a wonder that no one fell down a mine shaft that evening, so much alcohol had been consumed.

Doyle walked Lilly to her room in the hotel which adjoined the saloon. Lilly carried a bottle of champagne with her and gave a bucket of ice to Doyle as his share of the load. Ice was a rare commodity in Mogollon in the summer months, as it had to be stored deep in the mine shafts and protected with sawdust in order to keep it from melting.

The couple went into Lilly's room and the Marshal opened the champagne with a loud pop, the cork hitting the ceiling and ricocheting onto the bed. Lilly ran to grab the cork, thinking that it would bring her good luck. As she threw herself upon the bed, the red taffeta skirt she was wearing flew up baring her thighs. Marshal Doyle gulped as his face turned beet red from the blood rushing to his head. The excitement of seeing the flash of alabaster flesh provoked a state of anticipation that he had never experienced in his life.

Lilly recovered the cork, rolled over onto her back and sat up on the bed, fluffed her dress back into place, and said, "Let's drink to the future."

Doyle filled their glasses and, handing Lilly hers, offered a toast, "To you, Lilly, for this party and your friendship, two things I will treasure forever."

After the toast was celebrated, Lilly proposed her own, saying, "To you, Joe Doyle, my rock of Gibraltar. The one unfailing light I've known."

They finished the toast and filled the glasses again and talked excitedly about all of the crazy antics of the party guests.

Even Banker Wilson had been carried away, making a lengthy speech from atop the bar, pledging to the town, "I'll commission a bronze statue of Marshal Joe Doyle to stand on the main street of town to remind us forever of his contribution to our community."

Then there was Chuck Gifford, who ran the livery stable, who jumped up on the bar and said, "You don't need to do that Wilson, I'll be a statue of Marshal Doyle."

With that he struck a pose as if frozen in stone and promptly passed out, falling over backward behind the bar. The two laughed raucously as they recounted this spectacular event.

Joe Doyle allowed, "The old fool would have been killed if he hadn't been so drunk."

The two continued to draft on the magnum of champagne for three quarters of an hour when Marshal Doyle, not wanting to wear out his welcome, said, "Well, Lilly, I guess I'd better go. It's pretty late and it's been a big night."

As Lilly stood up, she looked at Joe and said, "I hate to see the evening end. It's been so pleasant, such a joy to be with you and remember all of the things we have shared and recall both the joy and peril we've known together."

As she looked at Joe in the soft light of the kerosene lantern, she saw a tall, strapping, handsome man in his late fifties, red hair tinged with gray at the temples, clean shaven, sharp featured, broad shouldered. It was almost as if she were looking at him for the first time, realizing how handsome he was. Purely on impulse, she stepped to the Marshal and threw her arms around his neck and said, "Bend over you fool, and let me really thank you. The Marshal accepted her embrace and lowered his head to meet her lips. It was no school girl kiss that Marshal Doyle received and he hoped against hope that Lilly was showing a romantic interest in him. Yet he knew that could not be. He had loved this woman it seemed like forever and she had never displayed anything other than platonic friendship toward him.

When she had not accepted his offer of marriage and married her bartender instead, he felt that he had been totally rejected. Joe didn't know that Lilly had turned down his offer of marriage because she didn't want him to be saddled with an unwelcome wife. She had asked her bartender to make her an honest woman in exchange for a partnership in the saloon. She felt that this way she was at least paying her way and would not be a burden. Little did she know how downfallen Marshal Joe Doyle had been when it was announced that Lilly had married Alfonse.

During the embrace, Lilly parted her lips but Marshal Doyle did not respond although he was clasping Lilly in a strong embrace. Lilly sensed that he was interested but holding back and, when she finished the kiss, she went over to the table and, cupping her hand, blew across the chimney of the kerosene lamp leaving the room in darkness except for the faint light of the moon gently streaming in the window. She walked back to where Joe was standing somewhat perplexed, and took his hand and led him to the side of the bed.

She sat down and, when he continued to stand there, she tugged on his hand and said, "Come on Joe, be comfortable."

Joe realized then that what he had fantasized all of these years was about to be played out in real life.

This was not a night of soaring passion and emotion but instead was a joining of two mature and caring persons; an assignation unlike any other Lilly had experienced. As she made love in the firm embrace of Joe Doyle, a happy woman, she had no thought of Whiting, giving herself completely to the pleasure of the moment.

In the morning, Marshal Doyle awoke to the smell of bacon and eggs and, opening his eyes, raised up in bed and saw that Lilly had ordered breakfast sent to their room. Lilly was sitting at the dressing table in a dressing gown, fretting with her hair when Joe swung his legs over the bed and reached for his shirt which had been flung across the bedstead. He hurriedly put it on and then grappled with his underwear and trousers, all the while not stealing a look at Lilly. When he has finally finished, he stood up and Lilly turned around with a big smile that immediately put him at ease and said, "Let's eat."

With that, the Marshal took his seat and ravaged the eggs and bacon and swallowed the large cup of coffee in a few gulps.

When he had finished eating, he stood up and, looking at Lilly, said, "Lilly, I don't know how to say this, but I apologize. I wouldn't do a single thing to harm you, and here I've done something awful. Everyone will know this has happened."

He paused for a second and, looking down at the breakfast, said, "Who brought the breakfast up? They'll be telling the whole darn town about this."

Lilly laughed and said, "I don't care and you shouldn't either.

What happened was wonderful and I wanted it to happen, and I'm glad it happened."

Despite this reassurance, the Marshal was still ill at ease and, spying his gun belt on the chair, quickly strapped it on and said, "I've got to go, I've got to go. Again, please let me tell you how sorry I am that I'm a damn fool."

Lilly tenderly grasped his arms with both hands and, looking up, said, "No you're not, Joe. You're an angel, and you're my angel. And what happened was wonderful. Thank you, sir."

Joe, almost clumsily with long strides, walked across the room and, opening the door, glanced back at Lilly and, half stuttering, said, "Goo - Good Morning, Ma'am."

After Marshal Doyle left Lilly's room, he strode to the head of the stairs and stopped and, looking around the balustrade, saw there were two miners talking to the desk clerk. He waited a moment and, when they left, casually sauntered down the stairwell without looking at the clerk who was looking very much at him and walked out the front door. He scurried to his office and made work by tidying the place up.

Postmaster Roberts stuck his head in the door and yelled, "No more orders for you, Marshal, how you feeling after the big night?" The Marshal bantered with Stan for a while and then, when he left accompanied him walking down the street until Roberts turned into Garibaldi's store to leave some mail off. At that moment, Lilly's buggy came down the street carrying her on her way back to the ranch. She was dressed beautifully in a blue and green dress with a black sheepskin cape over her shoulders. She waved gaily to the Marshal, blew him a kiss, and went on her way.

CHAPTER TWENTY-ONE

AMBUSH

Joe's appointment as Chief Marshal gave him authority to locate his headquarters office where he desired. He selected Silver City because it was a good central point from which to reach the various fledgling towns of New Mexico and Arizona that were springing up as a result of the discovery of minerals and a rush of homesteaders since the Apache threat had been eliminated.

News spread quickly throughout the Southwest that Marshal Joe Doyle had established a U.S. Marshal's Office in Silver City.

As was common throughout the West, the presence of a well known police officer who had a reputation for a fast draw attracted the twisted young minds who thought that killing a prominent gunman gave them status in society. Most of these would-be adventurers were hardly more than children and were easily disposed of by the Marshal and his deputies without there being any danger of loss of life on either side.

In many instances, a good long stare from the Marshal changed a youngster's mind about seeking glory by taking Marshal Doyle on in a gun battle. Occasionally, however, someone would show up who had to be taken seriously. Such a person was Perry Houser.

Perry was no star struck youngster but was a hardened gun slinging veteran of twenty-two years of age.

He had killed twelve men and all of his shootings had been declared legal either in self defense or while in the pursuit of other men as a bounty hunter. Chief Deputy Gibson had known Houser when he was operating out of Abilene, Texas as a bounty hunter. He had been working for the Pinkerton Agency tracking down known railroad criminals. Pinkerton had as tough a reputation as any organization in the West but they even became soured with Houser's brutal methods of hunting down his quarry.

On six successive missions he brought his man in dead, exhibiting a calloused disregard of life and a personal viciousness.

Perry had indeed forced each of his victims into a fight and, while he gave them at least a chance of defending themselves, the odds were heavily on his side. Had his real motive for killing the men been known, Perry would have earned the disdain of all Westerners as Perry really didn't want the problem of feeding them and staying awake, guarding them. The easy alternative was to kill them and throw the body across the saddle.

Some of the Western gunmen were natural born athletes and had speed and a sense of timing ingrained in them from birth. Others were of normal physical abilities but practiced day and night to hone their skills, both at drawing fast and placing a bullet on target. The third item in a gun fighter's bag of tools was attitude. A hard, cynical mind devoid of social consciousness was the real thing to fear in a gunfighter as it made up for any deficiency in natural or acquired ability. Ninety percent of a Western showdown was the emotional stress that preceded the shooting.

One of the things that Marshal Doyle always stressed when training a new Deputy to his duties was that the more they knew about the killer's mind, the better they could defend themselves and bring a criminal to justice. The Marshal told his men repeatedly that the most dangerous man to face was the one drained of emotion.

He would frequently say, "If your opponent is aroused, excited, afraid, or not sure he is the better man, then you have a great advantage over him if you, yourself, remember to shoot with your mind and not your heart."

When Chief Deputy Gibson reported to Joe that Perry Houser was in town, the Marshal knew he was in for an ordeal. Perry's well earned reputation had preceded him to Silver City. Not only did Chief Deputy Marshal Gibson know who the man was but Joe and the other Deputies had also been aware of his bad reputation. Joe looked at Gibson and didn't immediately respond to the news about Perry Houser. In fact, he walked over to the olla and poured a drink of cool water before addressing the subject.

"Russ," he said, "maybe we're in for one because, unfortunately, from what I've heard this is one of those kids who doesn't give a damn."

Russ agreed, replying, "Yeah, that's right Marshal. This guy's a bad one. Why there wasn't a cowboy in Abilene that would have a drink with him in the saloon and the only respect he ever got was from fear."

Marshal Doyle pondered the situation and decided that the best thing to do is to get a little information before deciding on how to conduct himself. He certainly wasn't going to run from a fight. But, on the other hand, there was no point in ending his career at this time in Silver City's boot hill.

He told Deputy Gibson, "Mosey on down to the hotel and see if he's registered and then just kind of hang around town and see if you can pick up on his activities. But leave your badge here. There's no point in provoking him until we know what he's up to."

It was a couple of hours before Gibson returned with news of his scouting activities. In the meantime, George Wilson of the livery stable had dropped into the Marshal's office to tell him there was a tough looking young man with a gun slung low asking questions all over town about how good the Marshal was, and wanting people to estimate his speed in comparison to other well known gunfighters.

George was a good friend of the Marshal and opined, "I tell you Marshal, this guy is out to lift your scalp, no doubt about it."

Joe laughed and affectionately grabbed both shoulders of George and shook him gently, saying, "By God, he'll have to pry it off, won't he George."

George was happy to see his old friend's confidence and said, "Okay Marshal, I'll buy that. I just wanted you to know this dude was hangin' around and he looks like a bad one to me."

The Marshal thanked George profusely and, as he went out the door, clapped him on the back, saying, "We'll be playing poker next Tuesday at our regular game in the hotel and don't think I'm gonna take it easy on ya because you gave me a warning." George laughed and waved to the Marshal and hurried back to his livery stable.

Five minutes later, Deputy Gibson came back with a similar report heightened by a personal conversation with Perry. Gibson had walked into the Apex Saloon to talk to the bartender and see if Perry had been in. Well, surer than heck he had been in. In fact, he was still there and recognized the deputy as being from Abilene.

He called out to him and said, "Hey, Russ, what you doin'? Do you remember me? I'm Perry Houser."

Gibson walked over and stuck out his hand and said, "Why sure I do. What are you doing here in Silver?

Perry put down the half empty shot glass and, with a slow, deliberate swallow, wiped his lips with the back of his glove and smiled and said, "I heard Silver City was one heck of a good place for your health and I just thought I'd come here and try it on for size."

Perry continued, "Russ, what are you doin' now? The last time I saw you in Abilene, I was with Pinkerton and you were a Deputy Sheriff. Are you one here?"

Russ knew his cover was blown, he faced the situation head on and answered, "No Perry, this is a Territory, not a State, and we don't have Sheriffs. We have U.S. Marshals, Town Marshals, Constables, and things like that."

He looked Perry straight in the eyes and continued, "I'm Chief Deputy U.S. Marshal for the Territories of Arizona and New Mexico."

Perry was obviously surprised and moved backwards perceptively but, never taking his eyes off of Russ's, he asked "You're working for Marshal Joe Doyle then, aren't you?"

Gibson responded, "That's right."

Perry then motioned towards the table and said, "Let's sit down. I'll buy you a drink. You're just the man I want to talk to."

He turned to the bartender and said, "Bartender, bring us a bottle and another glass."

The bartender turned to the back bar and picked up a quart of whiskey and placed it near Perry's hand. Perry took the bottle along with the shot glasses and walked towards the table with Gibson at his side. The two men sat down and remained silent while Perry poured a full shot glass for each. He then picked his glass up and said, "Here's to old times and a bright future for both of us."

Gibson responded, "I'll drink to that," and polished his shot of whiskey off in one gulp. When he set his glass down, he realized that Perry had only taken a sip.

Gibson looked at Perry and said, "Is there something wrong with the booze?"

Perry responded, "No, I just like to drink slow, like everything else. When you get in a hurry you sometimes miss what's goin' on."

Gibson knew he had made a mistake by gulping the full shot as Perry was already pouring him another. He knew that Perry was hoping to loosen his tongue and find out what he could about Marshal Joe Doyle.

When Gibson put the shot glass to his lips this time, he took a sip only and sat the glass down and said, "By golly, you're right. It ain't bad whiskey and it does taste better if you let it go down slow."

Perry saw at once that he wasn't going to be able to get his companion drunk so he went head on, saying, "What's it like working for the fastest U.S. Marshal there is?"

Russ replied, "Why, everybody likes Marshal Joe Doyle. He's the most popular man in the Territory of New Mexico." Perry continued to bore in, asking, "Is it true that no one has ever drawn faster than the Marshal?"

Russ shook his head and said, "Perry I don't know. The Marshal's really not a gun fighter. He only defends himself and then only when provoked."

Perry leaned back, his drink undisturbed, half-closed his eyes still staring at Gibson, and said, "Well, I suppose that a man can wait to fight when he's been provoked – as you say – but he still better be pretty fast to live. I just wondered if this Marshal Doyle is as fast as they say he is."

Russ realized he knew as much as he'd ever know from talking to Perry and, sooner or later, he might say the wrong thing. He picked up his shot glass, drained it down, and said, "It was good to see you, but I've got to get goin'. I'm supposed to be on duty tonight and I'm glad we got a chance to pass some time before you left town."

Perry got up along with Deputy Gibson and smiled proudly, "Why I'm not leaving town old friend. I'm here for the good of my health and we'll be seeing each other plenty."

Perry put his hand on Gibson's shoulder as they walked towards the door. Russ wanted to jerk it free and turn and have it out with this wanton killer right then and there but he was afraid he wasn't fast enough and that his death would be a useless sacrifice.

He told Marshal Doyle all about the conversation and his own emotions.

Doyle looked at him saying, "That's exactly right. Don't get yourself into a scrape when you have doubt about your ability. If you think the other man's faster, he's going to be faster. That's when you've got to use your head or you're dead meat."

Two days went by with Marshal Doyle staying close to the office expecting a challenge to be received at any minute. None came however. Marshal Doyle and his Chief Deputy and the others in the office frequently speculated on what Perry Houser was about.

That afternoon at 4:00, all the deputies were out serving summonses and citations which had come in the mail that day, when a local citizen excitedly came into the Marshal's office saying, "Hurry, Marshal, down to the Apex Saloon, there's two drunk cowboys down there fixing to shoot up the place."

The Marshal strapped on his gun and hurried down the street. He was preoccupied with his mission and didn't anticipate that the reported ruckus might be bait in a trap. The big man strode into the saloon, heading towards the back where two cowboys were loudly arguing.

He had taken three steps when a cold, clear voice rang out, "Hold it, Marshal, you and I have an appointment."

Marshal Doyle had never met Perry Houser or heard his voice but he knew for sure who it was that was hailing him. He also realized that he was firmly in a trap. The two cowboys at the end of the bar immediately stopped their argument, which they had been paid to pursue, and the Marshal debated his chances. He had entered the bar and started straight for the back.

The bar itself took up the wall to the right. He could tell from voice direction that Perry was both behind him and to his left. The Marshal, being left-handed, of course could turn and draw much quicker to the left than he could to the right. He knew the minute he made any effort to turn that he was a dead man and would not have any opportunity to effectively draw against his ambushing opponent.

The deck was really stacked against him. Number one, Perry could see him and he couldn't see Perry. Number two, he had to turn before he could fire and Perry was already in a position to fire. Three, Perry had planned the whole thing and thought it out and here he was having to react instantly to a bad situation. He thought that perhaps he could put his hands in the air and say "Don't shoot me in the back," but he discarded that thought immediately. After all, he was the U.S. Marshal and people expected him to prevail and not quit.

The Marshal surmised that Perry had to be standing there with his gun holstered. Otherwise, he would be an obvious murderer with witnesses. The Marshal decided to gamble on deception and he let his left shoulder drop and, at the same instant, he turned rapidly to the right and lunged toward the floor. As he did, his eyes faced the bar mirror for an instant and told him exactly where Perry was.

The flash view he had of Perry was of a man in the process of drawing. By the time the Marshal hit the floor, his left hand had swung around, filled with his pistol. His trigger finger began to contract as he was still falling. Perry fired his first shot, dead center of the space the Marshal had just occupied.

As the Marshal had thought, the minute the shoulder dropped Perry began his draw and he was so schooled in his shooting style that he continued through and placed a bullet where he had initially intended, even though the target was no longer there. Correcting his error, he moved his aim to the right contracting on the trigger but not before Marshal Doyle's bullet slammed into his chest, knocking him backward to the floor, and dislodging his weapon.

The young man lay there gasping for breath, staring up at the ceiling, seeing Marshal Joe Doyle standing over him with pistol leveled squarely in his face.

Although he was in intense pain, Perry tortured a smile from his lips, and said, "I'll be damned, Marshal, how the hell did you do that?"

The youngster then closed his eyes, took one last gasp, and settled into oblivion.

No one in the saloon had moved during the shooting and aftermath until Perry's last gasp. Then, to a man including the two cowboys who had been duped into being bait, they gathered around the Marshal, shaking his hand, all saying the same thing; that they couldn't believe what they'd seen. The Marshal had done the impossible. Everyone saw him as a dead man when the youth's challenge first rang out.

Perry Houser was buried the next morning on Boot Hill. His horse and saddle and the twenty-five dollars found on him were the undertakers fee for providing a coffin, digging a grave, and offering a prayer as the body was interred. Only two mourners attended the ceremony, Deputy Gibson and Marshal Joe Doyle. No letters were written home to tell about his death in the Territory of New Mexico. No one knew where he was from, if he had any family, and no one believed that Perry Houser was his real name.

As Marshal Doyle and his friend looked down on the wooden box and saw the clods of dirt begin to fall, Marshal Doyle wondered aloud, "What might have been if I'd had a chance to work with him before he went bad. I'm sorry amigo, I take no pleasure in this. You dealt your own hand."

The death of Perry Houser fed the grist mill of rumor and Joe Doyle, while still alive, had become a legend. There were many more young men out there with the fever of the gun running in their blood who would like to best the Marshal. There was one thing certain, however, and that was that no one would ever again try the Perry Houser ambush.

CHAPTER TWENTY-TWO

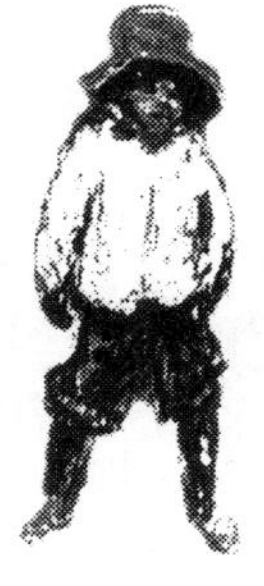

THE NEW DEPUTY

Two weeks after the death of Perry Houser, Joe returned from a trip to Tucson and was told by the livery stable owner, George Wilson, that all Deputies had left to go to a shoot-out taking place at the Paradise II mine at Cobre Creek. The Marshal waited until he could have a hot bath and a shave and a haircut before riding over to Cobre to find out what was going on. The Paradise II was located north of Cobre and, after a three hour ride, the Marshal reached the site of the excitement and found his Chief Deputy, Russ Gibson.

Doyle asked, "What the hell's goin' on here?"

Russ replied, "We got us a real screwball situation. There's a guy up there," pointing to the towering wood structure, "in that elevator tower, shooting the hell out of anything that moves down here."

The Marshal pressed his questions, "Why is he up there? What's goin' on?"

Russ explained, "Well, his name is Warner Tab and two years ago he was working at the end of a shaft when a mining car loaded with ore broke loose and came rushing down the shaft and slammed into him."

The Marshal visibly winced at the gory details relayed by the Deputy, and responded, "Hell, I'm amazed it didn't kill him."

The Deputy continued, "Well, it damn near did. They had to amputate his legs right at the hip. I mean he has nothin' left."

Marshal Doyle then asked, "But why is he on a rampage? What's happened?"

Deputy Gibson explained, "Well, the owners of the mine took care of his medical expense and have supported him for the last two years but they sold out to a new bunch from the East without making a provision for him and the new guys say it's not their responsibility; and Tab has taken it upon himself to declare war on the world."

Marshal Doyle was entranced with the idea of a legless man perched high on the tower, taking out his vengeance on a miscarriage of justice. He asked Deputy Gibson how Tab had managed to scale the heights upon which he was perched.

The deputy replied, "Hell, I don't know. Uh, he must have gone hand over hand up the cables. They say he has powerful arms." Gibson explained, "He moves himself around on a platform using his hands. He must have carried up an arsenal because every time anyone moves down here, volleys come pouring down."

The Marshal asked how many people had been injured and killed, and was surprised to hear his Deputy respond, "Nary a one. He's come as close as you can get without breaking skin but no one's been hurt yet. It's a miracle."

Marshal nodded his head saying, "Maybe, or perhaps he's a better shot than you give him credit."

The mine owners and other employees were holding a conference in the mine offices about a quarter of a mile away. When Marshal Doyle found this out, he went over there to see what their thinking might be. When he got there and asked them what their plans were, they agreed to a man that they needed to ring the tower with every gun they could get and perforate it to the point where nobody could be left alive at the top.

The Marshal told them that, "There'll be none of that. We're going to handle this without mob violence."

The representative of the mine owners was an Englishman named Jeffery Clyde who was adamant that the Marshal immediately proceed to return the mine property to his control and kill the crazy man who had interrupted their production.

As the Marshal walked out of the mine office, he thought to himself this guy Tab wanted them to do exactly that. Maybe this is his way of bowing out in a blast of glory, leaving the mine owners with the tab.

Doyle walked back to where his Deputies were and said, "Fellows, that guy up there doesn't mean to hurt a damn soul. If he's shot as close as you say every time anyone stirs, he's shooting where he's aiming and it ain't no miracle."

Without telling them what he was going to do, he said, "I'll be back just as soon as I can calm down Mr. Tab."

He turned and walked towards the tower, convinced that he couldn't be in better hands than with a marksman like Tab firing from his vantage point.

Joe hadn't taken twenty steps before the first bullet came whistling down to land at his feet. It was so close that the splintered rock barked his shins. Joe kept striding straight ahead without flinching or pausing. As he moved, a steady staccato of fire rang down from the tower and the lead splattered everywhere. As he strode forward, his confidence grew and he knew he'd been right. Mr. Tab had no intention of killing anyone but was bent on his own destruction and punishment of the mine owners. At least a hundred people had gathered in a circle around the tower, back far enough not to be a target but close enough to see this U.S. Marshal walking forward unscathed through withering rifle fire.

It took Doyle three minutes to reach the base of the tower and the firing stopped. The Marshal looked through the posts and beams, hoping to catch a glimpse of Warner Tab but was unable to do so.

He then called up, "Mr. Tab, this is Marshal Joe Doyle. I want to talk to you."

There was no answer. The Marshal then took off his gun belt so as to not to tempt fate and began to climb the ladder to the top of the structure.

It took five minutes to reach the wheel house perched on top which encased the sheaves that supported the cables. As he ascended into the house itself, he began to wonder if he had lost his mind. He had been right so far about this man not wanting to kill but here he was forcing him to the ultimate decision. Without wavering, Doyle continued up, knowing that he had to believe that he had made the right decision and act accordingly. For fear to overcome him now could be disastrous.

Without pausing, he moved over the last rung with a soft voice calling out, "Mr. Tab, I'm Marshal Joe Doyle, and I'm here to talk to you. Please! Don't shoot."

When he stood up and turned right, he saw nobody. He slowly turned left and there in a corner of the tower was Warner

Tab resting on his pelvis with his back against the corner of the room holding a 30/30 carbine dead center of Doyle's eyes.

Tab was the first to speak when their eyes made contact saying, "Hell man, you're crazy. I could've killed you a hundred times. You're the dumbest son of a bitch I've ever seen."

The Marshal, looking at Tab, replied, "No, I knew you wouldn't kill me. If you were out to kill anyone, it would have happened long before I got here. That hasn't been your game and it's not now."

It flooded in on Tab's consciousness that this man had figured him out and he laid his gun aside in surrender saying, "Okay Marshal, now would you like to figure out how to get me out of here without my help."

Marshal Doyle called down to the men below, who had come forward with the announcement that the shooting was over and told them to rig a bosun's chair and get enough rope to lower it.

As soon as Marshal Doyle secured his prisoner on the ground, curiosity seekers gathered around to see the man who had been raising so much hell in the tower. They couldn't believe it when it did turn out to be Warner Tab. They all knew Warner Tab as a bellicose malcontent since the new company had taken over the mine.

Marshal Doyle put the prisoner in a buggy he had borrowed and headed back. As they drove towards Silver City, the Marshal pondered his problem. He knew that Warner was certainly no criminal. Yet, he had violated the law and had to be punished.

When they arrived in Silver City, Marshal Doyle placed Warner in one of the cells with instructions to provide him with every comfort. The Marshal then took off for Las Cruces where the nearest magistrate was in session to explain his predicament. When he got there he told the magistrate, Lalo Schwartz, he didn't want to see Warner serve time, that Warner had been provoked beyond any rational threshold and yet he had violated the law and an example had to be made.

Magistrate Schwartz agreed, "You're sure right, Marshal, we'll do whatever you want. Can this guy do time in your jail in Silver City?"

The justice of this suggestion struck the Marshal full front and replied, "By damn, you've got it Judge. That's exactly what I want."

As a result, Magistrate Schwartz, a week later, sentenced Warner Tab six months to serve in a Territorial Jail without specifying the location. When the Marshal and his prisoner got back to Silver City, Warner turned to him and wanted to know what was going on.

"How come, Marshal, I've been sentenced to six months in a Territorial Jail. I should be on my way to Yuma, you know."

The Marshal looked at Warner Tab and said, "Warner, you'd cause so much hell in Yuma that they wouldn't know what was goin' on. You're gonna stay right here and serve your time like a gentleman."

Warner smiled and said, "Marshal, don't pretend to be tough with me. I know you're doing me a great big favor. It's just that I don't want it and I don't need it and it won't do a damn bit of good."

The Marshal smiled back and said, "That's my business, not yours. You had your day up on the tower, now I'm going to take a shot myself."

The six months went by as quick as you could draw a breath. Warner's cell door was never locked. He had free run of the office and the jail and, on his own, took over the chores of bookkeeping, administration, and everything else that was needed to run a Marshal's office.

At the end of Warner's term, the Marshal realized he had a problem. He had come to depend on him so much that he couldn't think of him leaving the jail and the job he was doing. And yet he had no authority to hire a man who was crippled. In fact, his instructions were that everyone that went to work for him had to be of sound mind and body.

The Marshal knew if he started writing letters to his superiors in Washington that it would be months and months before there would be any resolution. And even then, he was afraid it would be the wrong one. So he decided to stick his neck out. He had Warner submit an application for employment and where it asked for an accounting of disabilities the Marshal himself, in good conscience, wrote, "None."

A little debate followed and Warner told the Marshal that he didn't want to be lying to the federal government and Marshal Joe Doyle looked him straight in the eye and said, "Friend, when I say you're not disabled, it is the absolute, honest to God truth. If I ever met a man in my life who wasn't disabled, it's you."

Warner Tab took over the Marshal's office in Silver City and never was a federal office better administered than Marshal Doyle's domain in the Southwest. Warner had spent his life knocking around from one place to another before he wound up working in the shaft at Cobre, but under the veneer of Western adventurer, was a calculating, methodical mind. Warner had the Marshal's books up to date on a daily basis and made all the Deputies pleased as punch to be relieved of the miserable job of accounting to Washington for their time and efforts.

Warner was ecstatic with his new found position and influence. All he had wanted was to be productive. And here he was perhaps the most productive citizen in Silver City. Without embarrassment, he would hop on his wheeled platform and bounce down the rutty roads of Silver City to visit the post office, the livery stable, the hotel, wherever it was his duties carried him; the happiest citizen in the whole territory of New Mexico.

The confidence and trust that the Marshal had placed in Warner Tab had been paid back a hundredfold. No one ever had a more loyal, dedicated employee than the Marshal had in Warner and Warner returned the Marshal's warm regard with an appreciation that bordered on adulation.

From Warner's point of view, the Marshal was not a man in a million but the only man who could envision the real value that Warner had to contribute to society. He had railed against the old management and the new management of the mine to give him a task, to let him go to work, to let him with prove himself, but it was always the same. They looked on him with pity and gave charity. In the Marshal, he had found neither pity nor charity but more valuable commodities – understanding and trust.

The Marshal spent many a long night in the office philosophizing with Warner and finally confided in him of his great love for Lilly. Warner wisely told the Marshal to be patient. That if it was meant to be, it would be, and if it wasn't, at least he wouldn't suffer from anguish. The Marshal came to rely upon Warner, not only as a valued professional assistant, but a cherished friend; in fact, the only one he had really ever had.

In their evening sessions, the Marshal confessed his philosophy of life and his belief that everything had to be positive; that what was negative was destructive. Warner reinforced his thinking in this respect and told him how he had pondered the many hours of his recuperation. How he had reflected on the missed opportunities, the chances that were gone forever, the joy, and pleasure that would be no more.

And then he told the Marshal, "I'm really better off now. I have a viewpoint I never had before. I have a standard I could never have achieved. I have a will that will see me through any adversity."

Pausing, he added, "It's strange, but I know I'm a hell of a lot better man today than I could ever have been before."

These conversations put the Marshal on a high and he genuinely reflected that he had, in fact, played a role in this world, that his life had not been made up of meaningless bits and pieces. When he looked at Warner Tab, he knew that he had done some good, that he had made something of his life. This was a great feeling of satisfaction because the Marshal's other side was deep in sorrow since Lilly, with one exception, apparently did not return his love.

All of the efforts that he had made that he thought conveyed to her his devotion and desire had been unrequited. He did not know that she had never recognized the signals.

The association with Warner Tab did more to make a whole human being out of the Marshal than anything else he had ever done. Here was a person he had salvaged who was salvaging him, giving him purpose and meaning; teaching him the lessons he instinctively knew but needed to appreciate through the reinforcement of example.

They were quite a pair coming down the main street of Silver City. The tall, strong, handsome Marshal, the truncated Warner Tab on his platform with his arms pummeling the ground. And yet, everyone in Silver City saw them as the same. The two most decent, dedicated, God-fearing, hardworking human beings the town had ever seen.

One day, while the Marshal was on an errand, a killing took place at the Apex Saloon. Two strangers had been in a card game with three local cowboys when one of the cowboys, Chuy Lopez, stood up and accused one of the strangers of cheating. One of the unknowns had laid down a hand to claim the pot but it included the fifth ace in the deck. When challenged, the stranger stood up and placed a bullet right between Chuy's eyes.

Chuy fell backwards to the floor laying motionless as bystanders commented that he was without a gun. The stranger realized he had made the wrong play. With his gun still drawn, he menacingly moved toward the door along with his friends, indicating by flourishing his gun that the other patrons not interfere. The strangers slowly backed out of the room through the doors to their horses and the wide open spaces.

They took off heading north towards the Pinos Altos Range when they ran smack into Deputy Marshal Gibson and three other United States Marshals who were bringing a gold shipment into Silver City from the northern mines.

The two cowboys reigned up and Marshal Gibson suspected there was something wrong, and just then the self-proclaimed posse from town caught up with them, shouting, "Hang em! String em up! They're killers."

The two cowboys sat on their horses, not knowing what to do; the townspeople milling toward them from the back and the four U.S. Marshals staring at them from the front.

Discretion proved the better part of valor, and when Marshal Gibson said, "Come on boys, give up your guns," they complied.

Deputy Gibson then asked the milling throng, "What's going on here? Why are you in such a lather?"

The livery stable owner, George Wilson, who had seen the shooting, told Gibson how calloused it had been and why they were chasing the ruffians to bring them to justice.

Marshal Joe was back in his office when Deputy Gibson brought the two prisoners in. At the same time, the office was inundated by local citizens demanding that the two desperados be brought to justice as the cowboy they had killed was a very popular figure in town. Joe put the two in the large cell and calmed the townspeople, telling them that Warner would keep an eye on them and nothing would keep them from meeting their appointment with justice. The Marshal's Deputy and Warner had a big laugh over the concern of the townspeople, knowing there could be no escape from their calaboose.

The next morning the Marshal arrived to work before his Chief Deputy and the other Marshals. When he opened the office door, he knew something was terribly amiss.

There was no smell of coffee, no cheerful, "Come on in, here's a cup."

Instead, a deathly stillness greeted the Marshal. He grabbed for his pistol and crouched low, ready for anything that might come. Nothing happened and he arose and entered the room. He saw a horrible, grotesque scene – Warner Tab impaled upon one of the tack bars. The tack bars were three iron rods fixed to the wall to hold the deputies gear. Impaled on one of them, the torso of Warner Tab had been driven to the wall.

The Marshal tenderly removed Warner's body from the bar and kissed his dead friend's lips. Never in his life had he been so familiar with another man but in the shock and sorrow of this encounter, he reacted as never before. His mind filled with rage. How could anyone have done this?

The Marshal tenderly laid his friend upon the floor and vowed, *I'll get the bastards no matter what it takes.*

Looking at the scene before him, Joe reconstructed what had happened. The dinner tray had been pushed to one side, contents scattered. Obviously they had surprised Warner as he was passing the tray through the opening at the bottom of the jail door. No doubt they had both grabbed and held him to the bars until one of them got his keys and opened the door. Then they had made quick shrift of Warner by impaling him upon the iron bar.

Marshal Joe Doyle was enraged. In his entire life he had never been aroused to such passion. If vengeance could be his, it would be meted out with severity. This crime would not go unanswered, if he had to get on a horse and ride to hell and back, he would do it. The venom welling within him was not quenched by a few drinks at the bar. Instead, he waxed loud and eloquent before an incredulous audience who had never seen an emotion from him before. But, by God, this was one time the criminal would pay. No doubt about it.

The following day, Silver City buried Warner Tab, a man who had been a rejected criminal nine months earlier and delegated to the scrap heap of humanity. He was buried as a town hero in his rightful capacity of a beloved productive citizen. But all that was wasted on Marshal Doyle who was out to avenge the death of his friend. He had not liked the looks of the two cowboys who had been brought to the jail and had gone through the "Wanted Posters", but had found nothing that incriminated them.

Marshal Doyle was devastated. Not only was Warner his best friend, but a man who he himself had salvaged and he could not comprehend the callous way he had been killed. There were no bullet wounds, nothing to indicate that Warner Tab had been assaulted before he was impaled upon the iron bar. It was just a vicious act of extreme cruelty. The likes of which the Marshal had never seen.

The day after Warner's funeral, the Marshal headed out for El Paso to see if he could find any Wanted Posters there that would identify the felons who had perpetrated such a dastardly deed. He found no leads in El Paso and, after visiting with the local law enforcement people, returned to Silver City where he continued to brood.

CHAPTER TWENTY-THREE

FIRE

The summer of 1890 saw more forest fires than anyone could remember. By the end of June, the skies were black with smoke. The entire front range of the Gila was suffering from the conflagrations usually set off by dry thunder storms. The Marshal had kept a wary eye out towards the Pinos Altos Range as he received reports of countless fires started by dry lightening. Back in the Gila, the ominous haze told of the same situation existing in the very heart of the wilderness.

The Marshal hadn't been worried about Lilly and her children as the fire season progressed since the Burnt Wagon Ranch was well out of the danger zone. He was quite surprised when one of the ranch cowboys came into town with his horse in a lather to tell the Marshal Lilly had been gone for over a week. She and the children and two ranch hands had gone up Iron Creek to spend some time fishing at a cabin on a homestead Lilly had bought. The Marshal appreciated that Lilly might be in real trouble because the homestead she had acquired was on the main tributary of Iron Creek which turned and reached towards the Mogollon peaks themselves. He questioned the cowboy and found out every rescue avenue from the ranch was shut off. The Marshal left instructions for his deputies and, with the Burnt Wagon Ranch cowboy, made emergency preparations to head back into the wilderness.

With four pack horses loaded with gear, they were off within a half an hour, heading up Little Walnut and then cross-grain over the ridges to Corral Creek. They then struck downstream until they hit the west fork and then, after two miles, struck out to the left when they reached Iron Creek. All along, the skies were sullen from the haze of the smoke and, on the horizon to the north and to the south, they could see the glare of the blaze at night as it assaulted the Gila.

They had gone only a mile up Iron Creek when a spur from

the fire burning to the south raced northward and cut them off. They stopped for a while and then fell back from the intense heat as the fingers of flame crossed the canyon to the north of them. Within an hour, the fire in the canyon had burned out and the Marshal and the cowboy pushed ahead.

Two miles further up, they came to the cabin where Lilly and her children were anxiously holed up. It was with great relief that they saw Marshal Joe Doyle and cowboy Keith Terrell ride up to the cabin. Lilly rushed outside and threw herself on the Marshal, smothering him with kisses and then inflicted the same gratitude on Cowboy Keith as the children grabbed at the legs of both men, equally happy. They babbled all together, and told the story of the grizzly bear that had, they were sure, tried to enter the cabin.

"Marshal Doyle," the little girl Nakita said, "You can't believe how bad it was. That bear was trying to get in this cabin."

Lilly softened her comments, saying, "Joe, I'm not sure. I think the bear was as scared as we were. But, nevertheless, I was ready to unload this 30/30 when he took off."

The Marshal had seen wolves, deer, elk, bear, and peccaries all fleeing the fire as he had raced towards Lilly's sanctuary.

Joe asked, "Where are the cowboys who came up here with you?"

Lilly replied, "They left here four days ago to scout an escape route. Chet went upstream and Blinkers went south and neither has come back. We've been scared to death that the bears would break in and eat us."

He then said, "We can't wait here another second, this thing is coming down the canyon right now with a westerly wind, and we've got to get out."

With that, he threw the children on their extra horses, cut Lilly's remuda free and down the canyon they sped with the flames scarcely a quarter of a mile in back. When they hit the Gila River itself, they turned upstream to the junction of the east fork and the middle fork where, contrary to what everyone else wanted, they headed up the east fork instead of back to Silver City. Joe pointed out that the low lying haze which obscured the view to the south indicated the fire had taken off in that direction and their best hope of escape was to the north where the fire was burnt out.

No one questioned Joe and they pushed up the east fork to its beginning at the junction of Taylor Creek and Beaver Creek. Here, without hesitation, Marshal Doyle directed the party up Beaver Creek, and by the afternoon of the second day, they were in the Corduroy Meadows. They stopped to rest here as the conflagration was entirely to the south and Joe and Lilly reminisced about the time fifteen years ago when they had come through this very meadow, escaping the first onslaught of the Warm Springs uprising.

They rested for a day and then pushed on to the old stage stop at Frenchman's Well. Here they said hello to their friends, the Lujans, before heading for Magdalena. At Magdalena, they presented themselves as the first refugees of the fires to the south, which had occupied the attention of all the residents of the San Augustine plains. The grass was considerably grazed down throughout the entire area or else there would have been real panic in the plains themselves from the possibility of wild fires.

At Magdalena, Marshal Joe, Lilly and the children, and their cowboy companion took the train to Socorro and then down to El Paso and back to Silver City. A drenching rain had put out the fires the day before, so everyone could go home and back to their usual business. It was, however, a fantastic adventure for the children. And it was another notch in the tightening plan of capture which had preoccupied Marshal Doyle. It was obvious that Lilly was not going to accept anyone else, so why shouldn't he have a chance at this beautiful woman.

CHAPTER TWENTY-FOUR

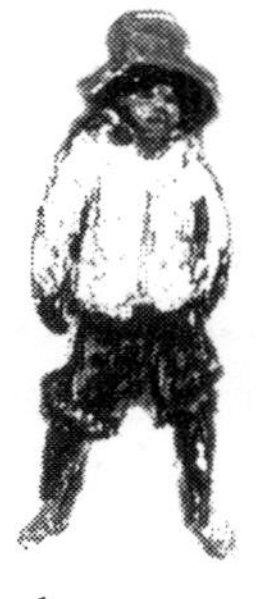

DEATH AT ADOBE SPRINGS

There was one family that was particularly a source of concern for the Marshal. Old man Rudd, the family head, was a venomous person who had been run out of Missouri by vigilantes. He had headed for the territory of New Mexico with the end of the Apache wars and was homesteading on Squaw Creek. He had four sons who were the biggest louts and brutes in the territory; totally uneducated and as mean and vicious as their father. Mercifully, the mother had died in childbirth delivering the last Rudd boy.

The Rudd's had bought a few scraggly cows and a couple of scrub bulls when they started their homestead operation but their real business was rustling from their neighbors. The oldest boy was Lem who looked like his father and had also inherited his father's shrewdness. If someone had asked him when he had taken his last bath, he would have had trouble giving an honest answer.

The second oldest son was Burnett who had taken after his mother. He would have had potential if he had grown up in a normal environment. But, as it was, he was his father's lackey and, not being too bright, followed in Lem's footsteps whenever he could. The third boy was Hyrum and he was a whining runt. No one trusted him to do anything and he spent his entire life trying to prove that he was just as mean and tough as his dad and brothers. As a youngster, he'd catch a bird and pull its wings from the body while it was still alive to demonstrate to his brothers how cruel he could be.

The fourth son, Jedd, was the cause of the mother's death. He was a gigantic person, six foot nine. He had been born breached and had caused his mother to hemorrhage. He had a dull intellect and passively followed his brothers and father in their various intrigues.

Marshal Doyle had twice gotten search warrants from the Federal Magistrate but on serving them on old man Rudd at their ranch headquarters, was unable to find any evidence of rustling. The only practical way to reach the Rudd ranch was to travel up Walnut Creek. Rudd always had one of his sons or a cowboy stationed at a lookout commanding a view of both canyons and had ample notice of every visitor. It was a simple matter to hide animals in the isolated canyons and Rudd felt very secure in his operations and expanded them to cover a wide area south of the Mogollon Rim.

They would pen the cattle they stole up in small isolated canyons and strip off the unbranded calves and kill all the cows that had brands. Occasionally they would find a cow or bull itself unbranded and these they would keep. As a result, the herd grew by leaps and bounds and soon was equal in size to any in the area. Their depredations had reached as far as the Burnt Wagon Ranch owned by Lilly O'Rourke and she called on Marshal Doyle to put their depredations to an end.

Marshal Doyle had again gone to Old Mesilla to secure a search warrant and, while he was on his way back, a rancher and three cowboys came upon Rudd driving off their stock. The rancher recognized the Rudds and a short gun battle ensued with no casualties. The rancher, outnumbered, broke off the engagement and hurried to the Marshal's office in Silver City. The Deputy in charge during Doyle's absence, Gilbert Lucero, got the other two assistant Marshals together and swore in three townsmen and struck out for the Rudd ranch on Squaw Creek.

The Rudd's lookout saw them coming and, as they approached the ranch house, the Rudds and two cowboys with them opened fire at point blank range, cutting down Lucero and his posse. Old man Rudd realized that time had run out and ordered the family to pack their essentials. With all the horses and pack mules in the corrals, they left the ranch, striking north toward the heart of the Gila.

The rancher who had reported the incident had followed Lucero to the Rudd ranch and was a quarter of a mile away when he heard the shooting. He diverted to a side ridge and watched events unfold. He could see that all of the posse were lying dead in front of the ranch house and that the Rudds were feverishly packing and preparing to escape. He went back to where he had left his horse in a thicket and returned to Silver City and arrived at the Marshal's office just as Joe Doyle returned from Old Mesilla accompanied by Deputy Gibson.

He told Doyle the horrible news that he was sure three deputies were dead and also the townspeople who had been deputized. Doyle gathered a small posse of four cowboys who were in town, including the rancher who had made the initial report, and struck out for the Rudd ranch. When they arrived, as they feared, they found the bodies of the posse stretched out where they had fallen in the first fusillade from the ranch house.

Doyle was crushed, he had brought Lucero along as an assistant Marshal, knowing he had the makings of being a great lawman. He had tried to instill in him the need to be cautious. To always shoot with the head and not the heart. And yet apparently he had failed because Lucero had amateurishly walked into an ambush. Lucero had been along on the previous two visits the Marshal had made to the Rudd ranch and the easy reception they had received on those occasions lulled him into carelessness. Marshal Doyle sent one of the cowboys back to Silver City to advise everyone that they were going to stay on the trail and that it headed due north into the Gila.

Marshal Doyle had brought his tracking dog, Arkansas, along. Arkansas was a nondescript mongrel that the Marshal had picked up in Mogollon as a stray on the streets. The pup had developed into one of the best tracking dogs in the country and, while he was of small stature, had the endurance of any working dog.

The trail led due north towards the Mogollon Rim which was the break between the canyons and mountains of the Gila and the Plains of San Augustine. Here the trail of the quarry divided. Old man Rudd did not know if he was being closely followed but decided to employ a ruse in case he was. He had divided the group and, with two of his sons, had continued north to the top of the rim, sending the others due east towards the Black Range with instructions to meet them at the Adobe Springs in Corduroy Canyon.

When the trail divided, Marshal Doyle divided his force and, with Gibson, stayed on the trail heading north and sent the others east towards the Black Range. Five miles past the rim, the trail turned to the left and was getting warmer, proven by the excitement of Arkansas. Marshal Doyle and Gibson headed west following the trail.

After a couple of miles, the Marshal reined in and said, "Gibson, let's think this thing out. Why would they divide and one party go due east and the other party go due west, if not to confuse us. Due west is nothing but wilderness for hundreds of miles, and due east is the Rio Grande valley and a lot of people who will be looking for these coyotes."

He continued, "I think it's a trick and that they're going to rendezvous someplace to the north, and a logical place would be Adobe Springs. From there they can move northward through easy country and disappear into the unsettled northern territory."

The Marshal acted on his hunch and immediately he and Gibson turned north, pushing their horses at top speed to reach the possible rendezvous ahead of the Rudd gang. They pushed their horses so hard that Gibson, coming down a canyon wall, took a bad spill and his horse strained a front leg and could not be ridden.

Doyle left him to walk the limping horse towards the Adobe Springs while he pushed on rapidly. In two hours Doyle had reached the Adobe Springs and found them deserted. He tethered his horse in a clump of pine trees a quarter of a mile away and positioned himself right in the middle of the rocks at the edge of the springs in order to control the open grasslands to the south.

He had been there about an hour when both Rudd groups reached the flats directly in front of him at the same time. They joined forces and rode together towards the springs to water their jaded mounts. All seven were abreast and Marshal Doyle had to make a quick decision. He would have liked to have stood up and told them they were under arrest and taken his chances if they decided to fight.

He quickly abandoned this plan as it would have been hopeless to have outgunned every one of them if he gave them a decent chance to draw.

He, therefore, waited until the nearest rider was a scant thirty feet from his hiding place, when he stood up with his carbine at the shoulder shouting, "Hands up!" He then opened fire as old man Rudd reached for his weapon.

When the carbine emptied, Joe cast it down and finished the job with both side arms blazing.

With the first shot, the horses panicked, the riders tried to pull in, and one by one they went down to the last man. Three of them got shots off in the direction of the Marshal but they didn't even come close. It wasn't the fairest gunfight on record but the odds evened it out and it certainly served the cause of justice, avenging the execution of the Marshal's Deputies and their posse.

As soon as the shooting was over, Marshal Doyle sat down on the rock he had been crouched behind and contemplated the scene of carnage about him. Here were seven men dead who themselves had killed five others two days earlier, all for a few rustled cows priced at ten dollars per head. It just didn't make sense. That loss of human life over such paltry value. And yet here he was, part of the code of the West, living out a violent role in a violent society.

Marshal Doyle thought, this just can't go on. It's crazy. This country is gonna have to gentle down to have a future.

His philosophizing over, Marshal Doyle got up and collected the gun belts from the dead. The Marshal went through all the pockets, putting wallets, watches, money, and knives and other valuables in one of his pack saddles for safekeeping. It took him a little longer to round up the surviving horses which had scattered with the fusillade of shots. As he was chasing the last one down, Russell Gibson entered the clearing from the south, walking his lame horse. Shortly, in back of him were the rest of the party which had split to the east at the beginning of the escarpment.

Everyone was stunned at the sight they saw and couldn't believe that the Marshal had single-handedly disposed of the entire gang. He retold the story a dozen times and still they found it hard to believe that a man with a carbine could put seven desperate men away without a scratch on him. He explained that it was a total surprise; that they were mounted; that their horses were bolting; that anyone could have done it. He also freely admitted that he was not too proud of his warning. Everyone agreed they deserved not the least bit of consideration; that he had given them far more than they deserved.

The misgiving Doyle had was quickly cured when Deputy Gibson called out, "Marshal, those guys with the Rudds are the ones who killed Tab and broke jail." Doyle walked over and took a good look. They had grown whiskers but, no mistake, they were the murderers of his friend Warner Tab, at bay, dead by at his own hand.

As the sun was slipping over Indian Peaks, Marshal Doyle directed his posse to place the dead men over saddles and packs and tie the hands to the feet under the bellies of the mounts. They started off by moonlight towards Frenchman's Well.

It was mid January and biting cold and the Marshal was determined to ride all night if necessary to reach the well. Things went a lot better than planned. The horses preferred traveling to being hobbled in temperatures of ten below. Even Russ Gibson's lame mount was keeping pace.

It was three in the morning when they reached Frenchman's Well and woke up Frank Lujan. Frank had run the stage stop at Frenchman's Well when the North Star Stage was still running. When the stage line terminated at the beginning of the Warm Springs Apache uprising, Frank had bought the property and gone to ranching. Frank was glad to see his old friend, Joe Doyle, who he had come to know well when Doyle was the Marshal at Magdalena some thirty miles to the northeast. He helped them take their grizzly loads off their mounts and they stacked the frozen bodies in a corner of the barn. Frank remarked they better put them back on the right animals as they were frozen to the shape of each particular mount. The men laughed at Frank's observation and they all went into the house where Mrs. Lujan had gotten up and was fixing a late dinner.

Again, Doyle was called on to tell of the shooting at Adobe Springs. Three of the Lujan children were still living at home, helping their parents, and they had also gotten up with all the excitement and everyone sat around the fireplace spellbound as the Marshal told his tale. There had been many spectacular gun fights in the New Mexico territory but everyone agreed this had to top them all.

As they were getting ready to turn in, Lujan walked alongside of Doyle and put his hand on his shoulder and, in a low voice, said, "Marshal, I can tell you're concerned about how you surprised the Rudds. You gave them all the chance they deserved. Why, they wouldn't have even faced you in the front if you changed positions. They'd have got you in the back." Lujan paused and then with emphasis added, "There ain't a man in this country who'll ever criticize you for what you did. I'm proud just to know you."

They slept until ten in the morning and, when they all got up, it was to a rousing Mama Lujan breakfast. Home-cured bacon and sausage, fresh country eggs, hot biscuits and gravy, a hot, steaming pot of chicory coffee filled the sprawling Lujan ranch house with a fragrance of hospitality that was irresistible. The men dug in with great gusto and tried as hard as they could to pay Mrs. Lujan for the wonderful food she provided and for the shelter.

She would take nothing for her efforts but, smiling, accepted their praise, saying, "Come back as quick as you can and visit some with the family."

Mr. Lujan proved right. The bodies were frozen hard in the positions they had been in while being packed and they had trouble matching the mounts. Finally, though, they were ready and they were off, a strange cortege plodding across the plains of St. Augustine. Lujan had provided some old canvas as shrouds for the dead men and the group could easily have been mistaken for a pack train of traders, hauling their wares to some outpost.

It was late afternoon when they pulled into Magdalena. They went directly to Marshal Doyle's old office on the west side of town and stored the dead men in the one cell. There were no prisoners in the jail and the office was now occupied by a town marshal.

Marshal Doyle went to the railroad station and found that the afternoon train had brought a box car and a passenger car along with the ore cars and there was room for the Marshal's men and their mounts and the dead men to go by rail to Socorro in the morning.

All the townspeople gathered at Rick Levy's small hotel to hear, again, of the amazing exploits of Marshal Doyle at Adobe Springs. No doubt about it, Magdalena had to be the most jaded town in the West when it came to violence. There wasn't any kind of a Western shoot-out that they hadn't seen. But everyone agreed this took the cake, and everyone jostled for a chance to shake the Marshal's hand and slap him on the back and tell him how much they appreciated having him as a peace officer in the territory of New Mexico.

The Marshal was offered drink after drink but turned them all down. While he was happy to be with his friends and accept their applause, he was also in a very somber mood, reflecting on the deaths of so many men.

He attempted to erase these thoughts, telling himself the cardinal rule of being a peace officer is to use your head and not your heart. *Don't get sentimental or you'll join the corpses stacked down at the jail.*

The train was scheduled to pull out at nine o'clock and everyone got up early and tended their horses and got the bodies down to the freight office where they were tagged and shipped with the horses to Socorro and then by Santa Fe rail to El Paso and back to Silver City.

The Marshal wanted the bodies brought to Silver City to be autopsied to clearly establish that they had been shot from the front and, also, to help in determining the identity of the two strangers with the Rudd gang. It turned out that they were desperados from Montana who were hiding from murder warrants in their home state. They each carried a five thousand dollar reward.

CHAPTER TWENTY-FIVE WHITE HELL

Marshal Doyle waved good-bye to his friends as they left on the train and, muscles creaking, got on his horse and, with his dog, Arkansas, left town heading due west. He gave Deputy Gibson a book of warrants to use for the expenses of the group and instructions about the autopsies to be performed in Silver City. He had decided that since he was in Magdalena, instead of taking the two days necessary to go by train back to Silver City, he'd ride over to Luna, New Mexico and look into a growing problem of conflict between the Mormon and Texan settlers.

With the end of the Apache threat, the Mormons were pushing across from central Arizona and rapidly taking up homesteads in the irrigable valleys while at the same time, and for the same reason, Texans from the central and western part of that state were pouring in, taking up homesteads mainly in the mountain valleys so they could control the water and establish ranches.

It was inevitable that the two cultures would come into conflict with each other. While they were both hard working people, the Mormons were very religious, did not drink or socialize in saloons or dance halls. On the other hand, the Texans were hard drinking, hard driving individuals who went to church under the open sky with a pine tree for the pulpit.

The Texans wanted the meadows to remain uncultivated so they would provide lush pasture for their cattle. The Mormons, on the other hand, wanted to homestead up these valleys, fence them off and keep the cattle out while they flourished on their farms. In the past two years, there had been three shooting incidents and the Marshal was getting more and more pleas for help from the Mormon settlers who feared a raid and massacre by the Texans.

Their fears were well founded, the Texans were planning a revenge on the Luna community for the death of a "Broken Metate Ranch" cowboy who had gotten drunk on a Sunday afternoon and tried to rape one of the young Mormon girls he found by herself, walking back from church to her family's homestead. Her brother came along and interrupted the attempt and, drawing a gun, killed the young cowboy.

The ranchers didn't believe the Mormon's story and talk was running high about a showdown. Doyle felt that the situation was explosive enough to deserve his personal attention and, since he was only a two-days' ride from Luna, he would go over there himself and save the extra days it would take if he went first to Silver City.

In order to make better time, the Marshal had taken two horses and rapidly pushed westward. It had warmed some, and masses of billowing clouds were blowing from the south, drifting from left to right as the Marshal rode along. He speculated on whether or not this could be the harbinger of a major winter storm as they usually started with moisture pouring up from the Gulf of California.

By 4:00 he was in the small community of Datil where he stopped for a meal and a chance to let his horses eat and rest. At 5:00 he was back on his way, in spite of the advice of the livery owner to spend the night and avoid the possibility of a norther hitting.

Marshal Doyle listened as the liveryman stated, "You know, this is how those darn things come, all that water coming up off the Gulf, and then that cold wind from the north, and we could sure get a blue norther out of this, if I know my clouds."

The Marshal agreed, saying, "You're right. But then again, its more likely to be an inch or two and I really need to get on over to Luna as quick as I can. Besides, I've got two horses and know the way, and have been in plenty of storms."

A couple of hours after leaving Datil it started to snow and the wind shifted from the south to the west. The Marshal felt secure but still, in order to play it safe, when he came to an abandoned ranch on the side of the road, he stopped to put the horses up in the corrals while he and Arkansas made a cold camp inside the remains of the house.

At 3:00 in the morning, a ruckus outside awakened the Marshal. Arkansas was barking wildly. The Marshal rushed outside into a blinding snow storm and saw four gray shapes circling the horses in the corrals. They were lobo wolves. Just then, the horses broke through the rotting poles and took off into the face of the storm which was now coming out of the north, with the wolves in hot pursuit. There was nothing Joe could do. The horses were flying at break-neck speed, so were the wolves and, unfortunately, Arkansas right in back of them. The Marshal yelled at the top of his voice, "Come back Arkansas! You don't have a chance with those Lobos."

Arkansas was a third the size of a lobo wolf but he had the courage of a lion and was determined to save the horses if he could. The Marshal called and called in vain. He finally went back into the house to wait for dawn and see what the weather would bring. When he awoke about six it was beginning to lighten outside, but it was also snowing more heavily. The Marshal went outside to survey the snow depth when, to his great joy he saw Arkansas limping across the corral. Apparently the little dog had caught up with one of the wolves and received a good thrashing.

The Marshal was amazed the dog could even have survived and said to him, "Little fellow, what's the matter with you? If you're gonna run with me you gotta fight with your mind and not your heart. You didn't have a chance out there with those lobos, thank God you're alive."

Arkansas gratefully licked Joe's hand and the two moved back into the house where the Marshal was able to coax a little fire from the hearth and they ate some of their meager provisions.

The Marshal surveyed their predicament and finally, petting Arkansas, said, "Old feller, we haven't got much choice. If we stay here, there's a couple of days of food left and then we're gonna be in big trouble. There's enough wood here in the house itself to keep a fire going but we'll have to eat each other to stay alive. I hate to tell you this, but I think we're going to have to go out into that storm and make it to Pie Town."

The Marshal continued, "It's gonna be a smart hike for us but we'll be there before our bellies even begin to grumble."

By the time the two travelers started, the storm had not increased in intensity and the Marshal was confident that they'd easily be able to stay on the road and reach the security of Pie Town.

Two hours later, he began to wonder if his good luck had run out. The storm had increased dramatically and it was now blowing the snow horizontally, drifting everywhere and totally obliterating any trace of the road. The Marshal was very familiar with the land, however, and was certain he was proceeding to the west and, if not on the road, in its vicinity. He could tell from the drainage of the canyons and the trending of the hills and of valleys which he was cutting at a right angle, that he was going in the right direction. His confidence was considerably shaken, however, when in another few hours they were suddenly in a flat area which was not familiar to him and he lost all reference as to direction. Two hours later, after walking what he hoped was a straight line, they arrived at a break in the plain and found shelter for a while in some large boulders.

Here the Marshal confided in Arkansas, "Partner, I don't know where the hell we are. We might be right back where we started for all I know. But we can't stay here. If we do, we'll both be frozen to death within a couple of hours."

With that pronouncement, off they went. The cold, biting wind was drifting through the Marshal's clothing. He could tell Arkansas was suffering, his fur was matted with ice and, on several occasions, Doyle picked up the dog and placed him inside his coat and walked on, giving him as much shelter and body warmth as he could. Of course he benefitted from the body heat of his friend.

The snow was now eighteen inches deep and the Marshal tore some material from the tail end of his shirt to make strings to tie his trousers around his boots to keep the snow from piling in. The Marshal had been cold and wet before and knew that frostbitten feet would put him out of action as quick as anything and that moisture would hasten the process. Even with the snow threat removed, his toes were beginning to numb and he knew that he and Arkansas were in real danger.

The thought crossed his mind; he wondered if he was being punished for giving those men so little chance. Maybe he was being called upon to atone.

The Marshal was not a religious man but he wasn't one to ignore premonitions or forebodings.

On the pair trudged; their travel rate slowed even more by the deepening snow. In places, the drifts were accumulating to three feet and were proving a significant barrier. The Marshal now was keeping the biting wind on his right, hoping that the storm was consistent and that the local topography did not change. He had no idea where he was, but knew that he had to keep moving. The energy drain was overwhelming and even moving at a crawl, he was out of breath and panting. Somehow he continued through the night and on into the next morning, knowing that if he stopped all would be lost.

He wanted so desperately to lie down in the snow and close his eyes and just sleep for a while and yet his mind was commanding him. *Keep going. Keep moving. Use your head. Use your head. You can see yourself through. Move, damn it, move!*

The Marshal's ability to remain rational and override his emotions with logic had pulled him through many a scrape but it didn't seem like there was anything that could pull him through this one and his strength sank lower and lower and lower until, finally, he decided he could not go on.

He desperately needed nourishment. He could get all the moisture he wanted from the snow but the drain on his resources had been such that he was fast running out of the energy it took to survive under these extreme conditions. In spite of his mind telling him that it was foolish, he stopped and crouched low for a minute and was ready to give up and let the storm have its way. Then his mind broke through the emotion and reminded him that there still was a way to make it. There was no sense in both of them dying. The warm blood of Arkansas would give him the nourishment he needed to carry on and find his way out of this white hell.

For a few seconds, a tug of war went on inside of Joe Doyle. On one side was all the love and affection he had for the little animal and on the other side was the cold and clear logic that there was no sense throwing both lives away. The cold logic that had preserved the Marshal on many occasions, directed his decision.

He reached into his pocket and took out his knife and opened the blade and, while petting the dog on the forehead with one hand, quickly slashed its throat with the other. When Arkansas felt the cold steel slash through his throat, he let out a yelp and ran a few feet away where he stopped and looked back at his master. Joe had dropped the knife and reached towards the little animal with both hands. The dog responded immediately and rushed to Joe with his tail wagging only to collapse and die in his arms.

Looking at the limp body, Joe abandoned all thought that he sustain himself with the little dog's blood.

Joe's emotions instead completely controlled him and as he tenderly kissed the still form and then tucked the little dog in his coat, he stood up crying out, "By God, Arkansas, we'll just die together. God, forgive me."

The tears streaming from the Marshal's eyes were frozen as pearls on his cheeks. By now his mustache was a solid bar of ice and he did not even notice that the strings had come loose on his right trouser letting snow drift into the boot. He mechanically pushed on through the snow, his eyes half closed with the lids and lashes caked with frozen moisture. He was on the precipice and ready to pass over and be with Arkansas as his body strength waned.

With only minutes of vitality left, he became aware that he had bumped into something and was being held back. The time had arrived that he could go no further and yet he didn't fall. He kept his right arm clutching the body of Arkansas within his coat, and with his left reached to push aside the impediment. Then he realized it was not an object, that he was actually being restrained. He thought, *Can it be death?* He couldn't understand what was happening to him. He was in a trap, he was under the control of some force but he did not know what it was. He could hear sounds other than that of the storm and finally realized in disbelief that there was a voice pounding in his ear, "Take it easy, you damn fool. Take it easy, we're trying to help you."

The Marshal's rationality reasserted control and demanded that he think. *You're being helped by someone. You're being rescued. Help yourself. Think. Pull yourself together, you're alive.*

The prodding of his intellect pulled him together enough to realize that he was, in fact, being helped by someone, no, by two men, one on each side, guiding him along, exhorting him to keep walking. Somehow he was able to respond and move his feet to keep up with the men who were supporting him. Next, he realized that he was being led inside a shelter.

The minute they were through the door he could feel the warmth rush upon him and he was aware that he was being lifted up and placed upon a bed. He could also tell that someone was trying to pry the dog's body from under the coat and the grasp of his arm. Desperately he held on. Even though he knew these were friends, he was determined to hold onto Arkansas.

The men who had found Marshal Doyle were sheep herders, Luis and Ramon Hernandez. They were eldest sons of Roberto Hernandez, the owner of a large sheep ranch.

The boys had been working out of a line camp when the blizzard had hit and had spent the last two days searching desperately in the snow drifts for sheep that might still be alive that they could carry back to the line camp.

It had been a complete shock when they had stumbled on the figure of Marshal Doyle trudging through the snow, his face a sheet of ice, his right hand desperately clutching his jacket and pressing it to his chest. They had a hard time handling him at first. He kept pushing them away and determinedly tried to maintain his course and direction. They had finally broken through by shouting in his ears, shaking him and, at last, received enough cooperation to get him to the line camp and inside and on a bed.

As they forced his arms aside and retrieved the dog, Luis said to Ramon, "Look at this. This dog's throat has been slashed. Something strange is going on here. I do not like this. I fear that we are with a man possessed of the devil."

The brother shook his head and said, "No. There is some explanation. I do not know what it is but he loves this little dog and when we bring him back to life, we will find out what has happened."

The brothers put more wood in the stove and took the Marshal's clothing off. They knew that it was critical to restore circulation to prevent frostbite and so they took snow and briskly rubbed him down from head to toe, noting from the blue color of his toes that there was already a problem. By then, the coffee pot was boiling hot and they raised the Marshal up and forced coffee between his lips. He was only barely aware that they were massaging his body but the coffee was a different matter; when its steaming heat reached his gut, he began to revive.

Opening his eyes he could see the brothers bending over him, telling him that, "You're okay now, my friend. Just take it easy. You're gonna be fine."

The brothers were speaking in Spanish to each other but using English when they addressed the Marshal.

Reassured, the Marshal closed his eyes, and was ready to drift back to sleep when suddenly he realized that he did not know what had happened to Arkansas and he tried to rise up and gasped out, "My dog. Where is my dog?"

Luis gently pushed the Marshal back and, putting his hand on his forehead, said, "Take it easy, my friend, take it easy. We have the little dog. Do not worry. Your friend is safe with us."

As soon as the Marshal had drifted off to sleep the brothers went out into the storm again to look for sheep, knowing that the Marshal would not need any attention, that what he needed now he was supplying himself, a sleep like that of the dead. Two hours later when they returned empty handed, the Marshal had not moved. They left Arkansas outside in the snow solidly frozen and fixed their dinner and went to bed.

In the morning, the storm had moved on and the entire world was a ghostly white, shapeless and formless. Another foot of snow had fallen by dawn and there were three feet on the ground at the line camp where the Marshal was recovering. When he woke he was able to swing his feet around and sit on the wooden bed frame upon which had been stretched a deer hide to form a mattress. His feet were in excruciating pain and he had a very definite impairment of feeling in both hands.

The Marshal, on waking up, accepted a cup of coffee from the brothers and then asked, "Where is my dog, Arkansas, is he all right?"

Ramon answered him, "The dog is outside in a safe place. Do not worry about him."

And then the Marshal said, "But tell me, is he alive?"

And Luis responded, "No Señor, he is very dead. His throat has been slashed from ear to ear."

The Marshal clutched the cup of coffee in his hands as he blurted out the story to his rescuers of how he had killed the dog in order to live and then had been unable to partake of the life giving blood.

"Madre de Dios," Luis exclaimed, and then in English, "We could not understand why you acted so last night, but now it is clear."

And again in Spanish, "Madre de Dios," crossing himself as Ramon did likewise.

The Marshal ravenously ate the simple camp fare of dried meat, tortillas, and corn gruel.

Luis told Marshal Doyle, "My friend, we are about ten miles from the main ranch house and I will go there to find a horse for you to ride. We have no horses in this camp."

Just then they heard a voice hailing them from outside and the brothers rushed out to see their father and another brother with spare horses coming up to the camp. Their father, Don Roberto Hernandez, was worried about his sons out in the storm and had come looking for them. He found something unexpected though, United States Marshal Joe Doyle, known to everyone in the territory, miraculously rescued from the storm by his two sons.

The brothers rushed back into the small cabin to tell the Marshal the good news, that a horse was already there and their father had come with another brother. The Marshal was overjoyed, and then quickly realized that something had happened in his life which he did not wish to be known by any, other than the two brothers who rescued him, and himself.

Before the father reached the camp, he extracted a promise from them to keep the story of the death of the dog to themselves. The brothers told the Marshal that the little dog was buried with a cairn of rock for protection and was guarded by a cross.

They assured the Marshal there would be no mention of the fate of Arkansas when the patron of the Hernandez family entered the camp. The father was amazed to hear the story of the Marshal's rescue and asked him to remove the socks the boys had given him.

He turned immediately to the Marshal and said, "You know as well as I what must be done and done now."

The Marshal agreed and said, "Can you do it?"

To which the patriarch replied, "But of course, at once!"

A pint of Whiskey was poured down the Marshal's throat and before the effects could fully take place, all of the toes of his right foot had been severed and only two toes remained on the left foot. Controlling the bleeding was quite a problem in this austere environment. The old man took his knife blade and, heating it red hot in the fires of the stove, cauterized the wounds. This resulted in a subsequent infection and weeks of treatment, but it stopped the gangrene which would have claimed his legs or his life if emergency surgery had not been performed.

An hour after the surgery, the Marshal was on horseback heading for the main ranch house where he stayed for the next two weeks, recuperating from his ordeal. On the third day the doctor from Reserve was able to reach the Hernandez headquarters and marveled at the top notch job old man Hernandez had done. He lanced the ulcers and left a supply of alcohol to bathe the wounds and keep them clean. He allowed that he would not have to return and that the Marshal would be fit to travel in no time at all. The doctor told the Marshal, "You'll be able to walk well and ride as good as new, but your fingers, while not gangrenous, have nerve damage and you'll never recover full feeling."

"In fact," the doctor shrewdly observed, "your gun slinging days are over."

CHAPTER TWENTY-SIX 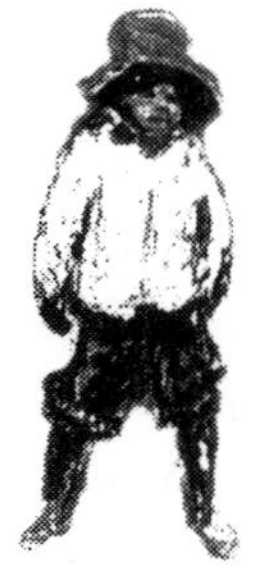 SILVER CELEBRATION

Don Hernandez insisted on personally taking Marshal Joe Doyle to Reserve in his buggy. The two men had become immensely fond of each other during the Marshal's recovery and carried on lively and animated conversation on the leisurely trip some forty miles into Reserve. They had never met before, but each man had heard of the other and they chatted like old friends. They quickly found they had a common view of the Indians and Don Hernandez confided in the Marshal that their family had resided on the western plains of San Augustine for three generations and had never had one problem with the Apache.

He told the Marshal, "We graze sheep in the summertime in their range, but always with their consent. We gave them lambs in return for the right to graze their lands. We never overgrazed their lands and treated them with respect".

He continued, "The Indians came to our house when they needed things we had and they never stole what they needed, but bargained with us and we always got along with them on the basis of a mutual respect."

Marshal Doyle responded, "I know what you mean and I agree with you, I fought the Indians because I had to, but I always did it with respect for their way of life and their land. You know, this really is their land."

Don Hernandez said, "Yes, I agree. It is their land, but it is also the land of all of us because really we are all the same. The war with the Apaches resulted from the blind greed of a few who claimed everything for themselves. You gringos call it manifest destiny. This is what forced the Indians to fight."

Hernandez then picking up the pace by snapping the reins, laughed and said, "But don't feel bad, Amigo, the Spaniards and then the Mexicans were just as bad. Perhaps there were just not enough of us to force the Indians to protect their way of life."

The two men philosophized the rest of the way into Reserve. Plumbing the depths of each others subjective thoughts, each benefitted greatly from the exchange.

It was late in the afternoon when they reached Reserve and checked into the hotel. Within ten minutes, word had flashed through the town that the great United States Marshal Joe Doyle was there, in person, with Don Hernandez. The town emptied and the dining room of the hotel became a reception room for the United States Marshal Joe Doyle who once again had to recount how he had single handedly fought the Rudd gang and killed them to the last man. For those who didn't speak English well, Don Hernandez acted as interpreter enjoying basking in the warm affection that the town's people bestowed upon the U.S. Marshal.

The two friends enjoyed a meal with the owner of the hotel and two of the town's leading merchants and then retired for the night. Early in the morning, the Marshal was down at the livery stable renting a rig to continue his journey to Luna. His conversations with Hernandez had made him all the more eager to reach his destination and try to prevent the outbreak of a real showdown between the Mormons and the Texans.

When the Marshal arrived in Luna, he was amazed. He hadn't been there for three years and was not prepared for the scene he saw. The entire valley had been taken up with farmsteads. There were irrigation ditches running everywhere and the stubble from last year's crops was evident on all sides. At the general store, he quickly parleyed with the Mormon Bishop who exercised authority for the Mormon settlers.

The bishop explained to him that, "The Mormon people want nothing but what is there right, and it is their right to enter upon the land and prove it up. No one has the right to run us off. It is nothing but greed that is causing this problem. And the greed is on the side of the Texans."

The Marshal listened patiently, asking many questions and finally rented a room from the owner of the general store who had three bedrooms for rent as an incipient hotel. The next day the Marshal received directions to two of the main ranch headquarters and traveled by buggy to hear the Texans' side. The same kind of a meeting ensued. He arrived at the Laney ranch about noon and they immediately sent their hands out to other headquarters to bring other ranchers in to visit with the United States Marshal.

They told the Marshal they had left the meadows as common pasture for the cattle of all the ranches and that fencing the meadows off in the lower country and setting up the irrigation systems crippled their ranching operations and threatened their investment of years of hard work. They pointed out how they had withstood the attack of the Apaches and now were being put under by people of their own kind who were taking up grazing lands that should not be used for farming.

Old man Laney explained to the Marshal that, "Texans are here by right. Texans were the first ones and it was greed that made the Mormons want to take away what is ours."

Again the Marshal listened patiently to all of the stories of injustice and outrage caused by the Mormon intruders, including the death of the young cowboy.

"After all," continued Laney, "everyone knows that the Mormons are sinful. Just look at their many wives. The girl must have provoked the boy. There is no other explanation."

The Marshal rode back to Luna the next day, having spent the night at the Laney ranch, and had a deputation of ranchers accompany him. That evening, in the general store, he visited with the two factions and told them his position.

He started out be telling them, "Gentlemen, I hate to tell you this, but in my opinion, this country was better off under the Apaches than it is under either of your groups but, be that as it may, something has to be done to make it possible for you to exist without killing each other and for that reason I am going to station a U.S. Marshal here to preserve the peace. I am going to cause a warrant to be issued for the arrest of the Mormon boy who killed the cowboy and the assistant Marshal here will be asked to investigate that killing and a trial will be held and, if it was a justifiable homicide, then the young man will go free. If not, he will be punished as the law requires."

There was nothing else the Marshal could do. Here were two groups of people each convinced that they were totally right and that the other group was totally wrong. The Marshal could see in the Texans, bigotry and hatred towards the Mormons because of their religious beliefs, and the Marshal could see that the Mormons would forever view the Texans as crude and vulgar louts.

Two days later, he left Luna with a heavy heart, knowing that the conflict he had just witnessed was going to magnify as everyone rushed in to make use of the virgin paradise left empty and undefended with the extinguishment of the Apache. The Marshal drove back to Reserve and picked up a new team and headed to Silver City. The only humorous thing that had occurred in the past four years was the observation of one of the young Mormon children he had visited with outside of the general store who had asked him what part of Texas he was from.

The Marshal wondered why the youngster had mistaken him for a Texan and said, "Why do you think I'm a Texan?"

The youth had replied, "Because you're wearing a white hat and that's what all the Texans wear. People from Arizona wear black hats. We're Mormons and we're from Arizona."

The Marshal humorously thought to himself, *I'll have to get a hat made that is half white and half black the next time I call a conference of these two factions.*

The Marshal traveled slowly and spent his first night in Mogollon where again he was mobbed by the entire town. Here it dawned on him that something very significant had happened in his life. He had always had a great many friends and enjoyed the respect of all who had been in contact with him but something very strange was happening with all this adulation and intense fascination with his termination of the Rudd gang.

There were many of the Marshal's old friends still in town and they regaled him with a parade in which the entire town participated. He left early the next morning for fear that he would be imprisoned again by the town's curiosity. He hurriedly moved on and reached the Burnt Wagon Ranch at the Gila Cliff Dwelling and was very happy to find that Lilly O'Rourke was there.

When Lilly recognized the Marshal driving up to the veranda of her sprawling ranch house, she ran out and threw her arms around him and smothered him with kisses, exclaiming, "Joe, oh how wonderful to see you. You don't know how I've worried about you. Let me look at you. Are you okay?"

The Marshal replied, "Don't worry, I haven't been hurt. I've lost a toe or two but other than that I'm fine."

They then went inside where Lilly had a bottle of champagne brought up from the cellar and put on ice. After dinner, they popped the cork and all of the ranch hands who had been asked to come in, gave the Marshal a toast and allowed he was the most famous person in the United States.

Joe spent the night sharing Lilly's home but not her bed. In the morning she insisted on riding into Silver City with him. She brought along her children and a driver and another buggy so that she could spend a few days before returning to the ranch. When they reached Silver City, the Marshal left Lilly at the hotel and hurried to his office to find out what the news was.

When he walked in the door, everything came to a halt. Two deputies that were there rushed to him along with three townsmen who had been filing a complaint. They pumped his hand and told them how glad they were to see him back at Silver City. Everyone knew of the close call the Marshal had had in the storm and were greatly relieved to see that he appeared to be in excellent physical condition.

Two days later Silver City had its very first parade led by the only five people in town who owned musical instruments, playing their hearts out in honor of this favored son who had made Silver City a safe place in which to live. As the parade moved down the street with the Marshal, Lilly and her two children riding in back of the proud musicians, the Marshal couldn't understand what was happening.

An act he almost considered cowardly had catapulted him into the pinnacle of fame. Another act which he viewed as the most despicable thing he had ever done had become a miraculous survival and had added to what he considered an illusion of fame and greatness. He thought to himself, *If there is a hell, I've damned myself to be in it.* And yet here he was being praised. He appreciated the warmth and feeling of his townspeople but the outpouring of affection of all of them combined paled in his appreciation compared to what he felt towards Lilly who was excitedly holding onto his arm with her left hand while she waved with her right to all of the townspeople lining the main street from one end to the other.

In the middle of this feverish excitement, the Marshal turned to Lilly and said, "Lilly, will you marry me?"

Lilly, without hesitating and continuing to wave madly, turned to the Marshal and said, "You betcha."

THE END

EPILOGUE

The Warm Springs, the Chiricahua, the Bednokohe and the Netdahe, man, woman and child, who surrendered were promptly imprisoned in Fort Marion, Florida. Even the scouts who had served the army in the final campaigns suffered the same fate.

After two years, the Warm Springs were told that they were going to move again. This time to a camp in Alabama where they would be further from the ocean and supposedly in country more suitable to their health.

On the appointed day, the Apache were assembled and taken by wagon to St. Augustine, where they were placed on a small bark and journeyed by sea down the Florida peninsula and into the Gulf of Mexico, landing at Mobile, Alabama. From Mobile, they went by wagons on a two day trip to Camp Mount Vernon where they were to remain for the next two years.

Tis-ta-dae immediately began making plans for an escape and return to the Black Range of New Mexico but put off the journey because of repeated statements by the troops in charge of them that they would soon be sent to Fort Sill in the Indian Territory of Oklahoma. The rumors proved to be true and, after two years in Alabama, the Warm Springs were transferred to Fort Sill where they were located in small clusters. The transfer came none too soon as Mount Vernon proved to be more deleterious to the Warm Springs' health than Florida.

On their arrival at Fort Sill, Tis-ta-dae tried to recruit other warriors to make the journey to New Mexico with him and to his great disappointment, found that no one shared his enthusiasm for the long journey. In fact, there were those that were pleased with their Fort Sill surroundings and the idea of owning an allotment of land. There were many who started attending the white man's church and there was increasing fraternization with the whites. In fact, it seemed obvious to Tis-ta-dae that the day would come when the Indians would intermarry with their former enemy.

Partly because of Tis-ta-dae's constant agitation, the Warm Springs began to petition the government for their own reservation. After several years of clamor, the army officials began to feel that they could consider reestablishing the Warm Springs in their homeland. One reason this was a possibility was because the mines had all played out and shut down throughout the Gila and the Black Range and there were still vast areas upon which public entry had not been made under the homestead acts.

In 1911, a group of six Warm Springs were taken by train to El Paso, Texas where they transferred to the Santa Fe and were taken to Engle, New Mexico, where they were met by wagons which took them to the old summer camp of Ojos Caliente. The group stopped in Monticello where they were met by the townspeople who had heard of their coming.

Tis-ta-dae, who was with the group, recognized members of the De La O' family and inquired about his old friend, Jaime, with whom he had escaped the attack of the great grizzly. He was saddened to hear that Jaime had been killed while riding a horse. He had just finished a long drive with cattle and had come to a cool mountain spring. He let the horse drink and made the mistake of not getting off first. The cold water, on reaching the horse's gut, caused a spasm and the horse fell over, pinning Jaime against a rock, killing him.

The people of Monticello had no qualms about the Warm Springs returning. They had never been engaged in hostilities with them. They had never coveted their lands, raped their women, or gotten them drunk to cheat them. The small party spent the night at Monticello and, early the next morning, started up the canyon towards Ojos Caliente.

Along the way it was obvious things had changed. The stream was no longer flowing. All of its waters had been diverted for irrigation. The great mountain of Cibola still loomed high overhead to the right but the Apaches were terribly disappointed in that the grass was not as green as they had remembered it. The party, unfortunately, was returning to New Mexico during a dry spell and the country was not the same.

When they arrived at Ojos Caliente, they were even more disappointed. The main spring had filled with debris from runoff from the adjoining hills. They had seen no game; no deer, no elk, only a few rabbits, and a mangy coyote had crossed their path. They did see large herds of the white man's cattle, which caused them to worry about the conflict that would exist if they were given back part of their reservation lands. They were certain that the whites would resist this kind of encroachment by the Indians. These cattle herds were owned by whites who were leasing the Indian lands from the United States.

They camped at Ojos Caliente for two days and Tis-ta-dae was able to visit the place where his mother was buried and he paid homage to her soul and power.

Tis-ta-dae was disappointed in everything he saw but still this was where he belonged. This was the homeland of the Warm Springs and he argued long and hard with the other Indians that they should all vote to return here and establish control and dominion of the ancestral land. He was sick at heart when he realized he could not persuade them and that they preferred alternate solutions.

Of the six, three wanted Fort Sill as their homeplace. Two of the others were desirous of accepting the government's offer and the invitation of the Mescalero to join that band on their reservation in the Sacramento Mountains. Only Tis-ta-dae still wore the blanket and wanted to be what he had been born to be, a Warm Springs living free on the land where his family had lived for generations.

When the group returned to Fort Sill, the Warm Springs were called together in a counsel and were told what had been seen. Again, Tis-ta-dae argued for the tribe as a group returning to Ojos Caliente. He was alone and the Indians split almost evenly between remaining in Fort Sill and joining the Mescalero.

With great reluctance, Tis-ta-dae went with the group going to Mescalero and, in 1913, he was with the Warm Springs who detrained at Tularosa, New Mexico and began the wagon trip up to their new home with the Mescalero Apache. Tis-ta-dae requested that he be assigned to the Indian crew that worked in the forest cutting trees, fighting fires, and protecting the habitat. This was the only job on the reservation which came close at all to his former lifestyle.

Tis-ta-dae would frequently make trips, when he was not working on his forest job, throughout the Mescalero Reservation learning the country. His favorite place was Sierra Blanca, the towering peak that reached eleven thousand feet into the sky. This was a sacred mountain of the Mescaleros and Tis-ta-dae was often alone on top of this peak tending a small fire, spending the night wrapped in a blanket, so that he could see the sun's rays in the early morning first strike the Black Range which lay just beyond the San Andreas Mountains to the west. It was a beautiful sight and gave him great comfort. And when he came down from the mountain, he always felt refreshed and invigorated. While he was not living in the Warm Springs homeland, at least he was able to see it and thus communicate with the ancestral voices that welled within him.

A strange thing now happened to Tis-ta-dae who had spent his life as a bachelor, not thinking about women because of the preoccupation with Indian survival. Tis-ta-dae had shunned social activities at Fort Sill as it was fashionable to mock the Indian ways. Many of his peers would tell him that it was bad to speak Apache, that the Indian ways were brutal and savage and should be abandoned. For this season, he had never congregated with people his own age and had preferred the company of the elders.

He met Isabella, a young Indian woman in her thirties whose husband had been killed in a logging accident. Her mother and father were Warm Springs Apaches who had taken refuge with the Mescalero and had been overlooked. As a result, they had not been sent to prison with the rest of the tribe. She was working in the Indian hospital on the reservation and Tis-ta-dae met her when a log rolled over on his foot and smashed two of his toes. She was a strong person of comely features and had faith in the old ways. Tis-ta-dae courted her at every opportunity and knew that this interest was returned.

He finally got the courage to speak to her father. Even though she had been married already, the Indian tradition was still strong that the parents would decide who the son and daughter would marry and negotiate the marriage settlement. In this case, the girl's parents were pleased that Tis-ta-dae would want to marry their daughter because Tis-ta-dae had obtained a position of respect in the Mescalero community. He was one of the few braves surviving who had fought with both Victorio and Nana. Of course, his fierce countenance because of the broken jaw evoked awe in itself. And then the story was told time and time again to the young Indian children about Tis-ta-dae's experience with the grizzly bear. By now the tale had grown far beyond what had actually occurred. Tis-ta-dae was viewed as a very important man.

After the wedding ceremony, Tis-ta-dae and Isabella received permission to leave the reservation and spend two weeks camping in the Black Range which they reached via train to El Paso, then to Engle, and then on foot to Hot Springs, New Mexico, and the Black Range.

Tis-ta-dae and his bride went up to Alamosa Canyon to the upper reaches where the grass was green and the water swift and cool. Two of the happiest weeks of Tis-ta-dae's life were spent here learning to know this wonderful woman who now shared his life and drawing strength and commitment from the environment. He frequently thought of staying here and not returning to the reservation. But then that would not be practical or fair to his beloved Isabella.

Isabella bore Tis-ta-dae three children. One of whom was a boy whom they named Nana in honor of the great Apache Chieftain. For the first time in his life, Tis-ta-dae settled into a normal pattern of existence. He was happily married. He had beautiful children. He had a job that kept him in the open throughout the day. And he had the Sierra Blanca where he could take refuge and gaze westward at the land that was sacred to him.

And so life went on for Tis-ta-dae, happy, content, respected by his peers, and loved by his family. And, as he grew older, Tis-ta-dae became noted as a tribal elder who knew the ways of the old ones. Whenever he could, Tis-ta-dae would gather the young Indian children around him, particularly his grandchildren, and tell them of the old ways and the importance of Indian values. How they loved to hear his stories of what it was like to be truly free, living in harmony with nature. They were excited by Tis-ta-dae's accounts of the tremendous feats and exploits of the Apache braves in fighting for their birthright. He taught young people how to make bows, how to make the fire sticks and work a piece of stone until it became a tool.

Tis-ta-dae knew that he had been born in the summer when there was a full moon and, because of this, he would attempt every year to visit Sierra Blanca in the summer when there was a full moon. In his ninetieth year he asked that his grandchildren assist him in the climb.

It was an arduous path to the top, climbing along a rocky trail past the timber line. Tis-ta-dae, however, was amazingly agile for his age, although he did walk with a cane and occasionally had to be helped by his grandchildren over a particularly rough place.

Tis-ta-dae's grandchildren were Netset, named after Tis-ta-dae's mother, a girl of twelve who had the typical Apache frame, very strong, and possessing great athletic ability. Tis-ta-dae's grandson was Chubascito, a boy of nine who was destined to be taller than most Apaches and, as a result, more slender, a gifted athlete with a keen interest in the ways of the old people. Tis-ta-dae doted upon him and saw in him himself as a young boy so many years ago.

The third grandchild was a girl by the name of Shufa who was different from the other two, more delicate and destined to be a beauty by any standard, Indian or European. She incessantly chattered and tugged at her grandpa's elbow whenever she was in his company, asking him questions about this and that to the great pleasure of Tis-ta-dae who, above all else, wanted his grandchildren to be "real Indians" and not just Indians. To Tis-ta-dae, being of Indian blood meant you were an Indian. Believing in all of the mysteries and lore of Indian heritage differentiated you and made you a "real Indian." To Tis-ta-dae, the blood was not as important as the attitude.

They arrived near the top of the mountain at Tis-ta-dae's favorite place near noon. Because of the altitude, there was a chill in the air. They had brought some kindling and fire sticks along with which to build a fire and, with it burning brightly, Tis-ta-dae had his grandchildren look out with him to the west. He pointed out the San Mateo Mountains as the northern limit of the Warm Springs homeland. Then he pointed to the mountain of Cibola, the southern peak of the San Mateo, and said, "There is Ojos Caliente, the main camp of the Warm Springs at the foot of the mountain. Your great grandmother is buried there."

He then pointed to the Black Range and recounted the experience he had had with a grizzly bear; and then pointing to a smudge on the horizon, said, "That place is called Black Mountain, it is near Camp Sherman where I was with Nana on a raid for horses."

He pointed out the Floridas to the south which jutted into Mexico and, in the far distance, the Chiricahua Stronghold and the Dragoons, and told them, "Beyond there is the home of the Netdahe, the wildest of the Apache."

He then pointed toward the south to Sierra de la Vieja and said, "In the distance beyond, and not visible even at this height, is Tres Castillos where Victorio was killed."

He then charged them, "Look and remember, some day the whites will leave this country and the Warm Springs will return to what is theirs. I give you the responsibility of remembering where it is we belong so that you can pass it to your children and to their children so that always there will be a Warm Springs Indian who can take our people home again. But I must warn you," he continued, "it will not be easy. We as Indians have a terrible of enemy. It has destroyed great numbers of your people."

He then recounted for them the tale of the massacre of the Warm Springs at Ramos in Old Mexico in the middle of the nineteenth century. He told them of the ignominious fate of great Apache leaders such a Juh who died in a drunken stupor falling off his horse on a mountain trial. He told them about his own father killed in a drunken brawl with another Indian. He told his grandchildren that the Indian could not tolerate alcohol and to avoid it above all else and to encourage their families and friends to do likewise in order to be prepared to carry out their trust and obligation to the Indian people.

His voice was cracking and tears welled in his eyes, an unusual display of emotion for Tis-ta-dae. He told them how Indian hatred of Indian and Indian fear of Indian and Indian mistrust of Indian did more to bring an end to Indian sovereignty than any other factor. He told his grandchildren, "The whites never could have followed the Indians into our mountain hiding places. Never could they have survived on the desert floor and pursued us. They would have been helpless but for the Apaches that led the whites and became their eyes."

As the warmth of the afternoon dissipated, so did Tis-ta-dae's strength and his final instruction to his grandchildren was, "Remember this! You were born an Indian. You must die an Indian! You must pass on the obligation which I, in my turn, give to you! Treat every living thing with respect and when some day the land is returned to us, become not only the ones who use it but those who also guard and protect it. These are the things that my life and the teachings of the elders have revealed to me as the truth."

Tis-ta-dae told the grandchildren to go back down the mountain and come for him in the morning; that he wanted to spend the night alone. They didn't want him to. They wanted him to come home with them. But he had two blankets with him and the fire was still burning bright. He told them that he would be all right. And so they reluctantly went back down the mountain as he commanded. In the morning they hurriedly dressed, ate their breakfast, and scurried up the two-hour trail to help their beloved grandfather come down from his mountain.

When they arrived at Tis-ta-dae's camp, the fire was out and the embers were cold. The old man was dead. He was facing west with his eyes open.

The children knew what they must do, spending the next two hours tenderly piling a cairn of rock about the old man and then they left him alone. They went back down the mountain to tell their family and friends that Tis-ta-dae, a Warm Springs Apache, was dead.

ORDER FORM

Please send me (_____) copies of
RIMFIRE
by Tom Diamond.

I am enclosing my check (#_____)
or Money Order (#____________________)
payable to Beaverhead Lodge Press
in the amount of $_________.*

Price per book:	$ 9.95
Shipping and handling for each book:	$ 5.00
*TOTAL PER BOOK:	$14.95**

**Add applicable Sales Tax.
(For multiple copies shipped to the same address, $13.95 per book.)

SHIP TO:

Name: ____
Address: ____
____
City: ____________________ State: ______ Zip: ______
Phone Number: ________________________________

Mail this form with your check or Money Order to:

BEAVERHEAD LODGE PRESS
H. C. Box 446
Burnt Cabin, Beaverhead
Winston, New Mexico 87943